and against him. He was wet and still sitting there, staring into his embracing ...

BY THE BOOK

Christine Dorsey

A KISMET ™ Romance

METEOR PUBLISHING CORPORATION
Bensalem, Pennsylvania

To Nicolette Reinert who always believed in this book.
Friendship will survive the miles.

CHRISTINE DORSEY

Christine Dorsey lives in Richmond, Virginia with
her husband, Chip (her one man critique group), their
sons, Ben and Christopher, and daughter, Elizabeth.
A former teacher of learning disabled children, she
enjoys writing and sharing the stories that spin around
in her head. Published in contemporary and historical
romance, Christine loves to hear from romance readers.

ONE

A fish?

Charlotte Handley rested her elbows on the wooden top of the ninth grade desk and peered around the wide girth of the woman in front of her. Sure enough, her eyes hadn't deceived her. When Charlotte had crept into Mr. McQuade's classroom—late—for his back to school presentation, she'd thought she'd glimpsed a fish before sliding into the only available seat, the one in the back of the room. And she had. Hanging around Mr. McQuade's neck was a fish.

The first genuine smile of a long evening, curved her lips as she studied the underwater creature worn by her daughter's freshman English teacher. The tail, a blue-green scaly point, barely grazed the narrow waist of Mr. McQuade's khaki pants. From there, the fish's iridescent body traveled up the teacher's flat stomach and amazingly wide breadth of chest to form the head and a fish-gape mouth just below a neat Windsor knot.

"Some of you appear curious about my tie."

The deep masculine voice brought Charlotte's attention for the first time to Mr. McQuade's face. His eyes were the same blue-green as his tie, and they stared straight at her. Charlotte felt the blood rush to her cheeks and cursed the fair complexion that would make her blush so obvious. Clearly, Mr. McQuade noticed her embarrassment, for he gave her a quick, crooked grin, revealing a matched set of sexy dimples, before looking away.

Charlotte released her pent-up breath slowly and forced herself not to slink down in the hard seat. Was it obvious to Elizabeth's teacher that she hadn't heard a word of his presentation because she'd been ogling his fish? What if he thought she'd been ogling him, too? Charlotte realized reluctantly that she had noticed the masculine body the tie covered. She *had* ogled her daughter's teacher! This self admission brought a fresh surge of heat to her face.

Well, one thing was certain. Charlotte no longer had to wonder why Mr. McQuade was Elizabeth's favorite teacher—the only one who could coax As from her daughter. This man's smile could coax hungry worms from their apples. Of course, it shouldn't be that difficult for Elizabeth to do well in school. She'd always excelled—until this year.

A mantel of guilt, never far enough away for comfort, began draping long tentacles around Charlotte, and her shoulders shook slightly in an effort to dispel the feeling. This was not the time to worry if she'd done the right thing.

Mr. McQuade capsulized the unit he would teach on creative writing, and Charlotte, as if in atonement for her earlier lack of interest in his talk, gave him her full attention. It wasn't difficult. He spoke with an easy, laid-back style that demonstrated how familiar he was with his topic. And even though writing was something Charlotte was not particularly fond of—as witnessed by her own difficulties with the English class she took at William and Mary—she found his idea of keeping a daily journal intriguing.

"Any questions?" Mr. McQuade leaned his hip against the corner of the teacher's desk and glanced at his watch. "We have a few minutes before the final bell of the evening rings. Then you can all escape this torture your children have to endure every day." He smiled and his gaze found Charlotte's for a moment before she looked away.

"I have one." The heavyset woman in front of Charlotte spoke and raised her hand until the teacher acknowledged her with a nod. "Why *did* you wear that tie tonight?"

Mr. McQuade threw back his head, laughing, and the deep, rumbling vibrations seemed to tickle the length of Charlotte's spine.

"I'm glad someone had the nerve to ask that." Again his gaze rested on Charlotte; again she broke the contact. "This," his long slender fingers played with the fish as he spoke, "is my first day of school tie. I wear it to break the ice, so to speak. The first year of high school can be scary—so can English. I don't want the kids to be afraid of me."

"Is that why you wore it tonight, so we wouldn't be scared?" The other parents laughed along with the teacher and the grayhaired lady who'd asked the question.

"No." He looked at Charlotte again and she began wondering if her curly red hair stuck out at strange angles or if she'd smudged the makeup around her large, blue eyes. Granted there hadn't been much time to get ready for the "meet the teacher" night when she'd gotten home from her job at the college library, but she'd thought she appeared presentable enough. Mr. McQuade's constant staring made her uncertain. Her innocent, girl-next-door looks didn't usually warrant men's second glances. Especially men who looked like Mr. McQuade.

"I wore the tie tonight because I lost a bet. One of your children—who will remain nameless—bet me she'd make an A on her first test. She did. I lost— sort of," he added, smiling. "And so I had to face the parents wearing a fish."

Elizabeth. An image of her daughter's grinning face as Charlotte had raved about her English test grade flashed across Charlotte's mind. The "you win" written in big, bold letters beside the A+ now made sense.

The bell rang, a loud obnoxious sound that brought back memories of Charlotte's own high school days. Most of the parents surged forward to meet Mr. McQuade and, no doubt, put in a good word for their child. But not Charlotte. She'd had enough of talking to teachers tonight.

Even though this evening was not to be used for conferences, several of Elizabeth's teachers had found a moment to let Charlotte know how disappointed they were in Elizabeth's grades. The last one, a Miss Zeller, had kept Charlotte so long, she'd been late for her visit to her daughter's English class. Charlotte had to admit the woman seemed like a real shrew. No wonder Elizabeth hated algebra. But disliking the teacher was no reason to be making Ds—a fact that Charlotte was going to have to convey to her daughter immediately.

With a sigh, Charlotte slipped her purse strap over her shoulder and started for the door, but a bulletin board covered with students' work caught her eye: "My Summer Vacation." The words sprang up at her from the tops of a multitude of ragged-edged notebook paper compositions. Systematically, Charlotte scanned the headings till she found the one she sought. Elizabeth Handley. The name was written above the date in her daughter's familiar script.

The report was direct and to the point—like Elizabeth. It described the move from their large West End Richmond home to the small two bedroom house they'd bought in Williamsburg, Virginia. It told of the leaky plumbing, the weeks of painting, and the flower garden that had resisted both mother's and daughter's attempts to make it bloom. There were no recriminations, no regrets mentioned. Just a listing of events. Even the trip to Virginia Beach that Charlotte had been ill able to afford, but that Elizabeth had seemed to enjoy, was chronicled in the same unemotional narrative that tore at Charlotte's heart.

She was uncertain how long she stood beside the cork board, but when she turned to leave, a now familiar voice stopped her. "Mrs. Handley, may I speak with you a moment?"

Charlotte glanced over her shoulder. The room had emptied. Mr. McQuade was escorting the last two people to the door. The mother and father were assuring him that they would stay on top of their son's homework. Regretting that she hadn't made her retreat when she'd had the chance, yet now unwilling to be rude to her daughter's teacher by leaving, Charlotte feigned interest in a time line of American authors on the board as she waited.

"You enjoy Hawthorne?"

"What?" Charlotte turned. Mr. McQuade leaned against the doorjamb, studying her.

"Hawthorne," he repeated, uncrossing his arms and pointing to the picture of the nineteenth century author on the chart. "You seemed to be fascinated by him."

Hawthorne? Charlotte looked back at the chart and noticed the name for the first time. Is that where she'd been staring? She remembered reading *The Scarlet Letter* in college and enjoying it, but that was a far cry from fascination. "Well, yes I do like him, I mean I . . ." Charlotte stopped short, realizing she was babbling worse than a teenager. What was it about this man that made her feel like one? She was thirty-four years old for heaven's sake. Too old to be gushing over a man, even if he was attractive—well, maybe she found his sensual lips, slightly pugnacious, no-nonsense nose, and sun-streaked brown hair more than just attractive. Still, he was Elizabeth's teacher and she was her mother—period.

"You wished to speak with me?" There was no reason to evade the issue.

"Yes, I'd like to arrange a conference with you to discuss Elizabeth's progress." He seemed as adept at getting to the point as she.

"But I thought she was doing so well in English."

Charlotte didn't mention that this was the only class that held that claim to fame. His next words told her she didn't have to.

"I'm also Elizabeth's advisor."

"I see." Charlotte readjusted the shoulder strap of her purse. "When would you like to meet?"

Before he could answer, a custodian pushing a rolling cart of cleaning supplies stopped by the door. He paused when he saw Charlotte standing in the room. "Sorry, Mr. McQuade. I thought you was finished in here."

"We are, Joe." Mr. McQuade motioned Charlotte out the door. "Come on, I'll walk you to your car."

"That's not necessary," Charlotte mumbled as he grabbed his sports jacket off the back of his chair and followed her from the classroom. She tried not to notice the soapy clean way he smelled. She tried not to notice anything about him. But it was almost impossible. In annoyance Charlotte realized she hadn't been this aware of a man in years—maybe ever.

"It really isn't necessary for you to walk with me," Charlotte reiterated, turning abruptly to face him in the now empty locker-lined hallway. She ignored the surprised lift of his straight dark brows. "If you'd just tell me a time that would be convenient for you to meet, I'll be there."

"You can meet me whenever I say? I thought you had such a hectic schedule," he said.

Mr. McQuade had continued walking toward the dark green double doors, and Charlotte had no recourse but to follow. His long-legged stride made catch-up difficult. "I am busy, but nothing is more important to me than . . . Wait a minute." This time he did stop. "How do you know about my schedule?"

He shrugged, the motion lifting the jacket held negligently over his shoulder by one finger. "Elizabeth mentioned it."

That's what she'd been afraid of. Charlotte wondered what else her daughter had told this teacher-confidant. She almost had to bite her tongue to keep from asking. Instead she tilted her head to look him straight in the eye, keeping her own blue ones steady. "Name the day."

"Friday." He pushed open the door and stood aside for her to precede him outside.

The cool autumn air wafted across Charlotte's heated cheeks and she took a deep steadying breath.

Friday. Charlotte's mind raced. After challenging him to name the day, she'd walk barefoot over hot coals before backing out, but he couldn't have picked a worse time. Friday afternoon was her English class and though normally she could cut it in a pinch, this week her first paper was due. "I'll ask professor Wyatt if I can leave early."

Charlotte didn't realize she'd spoken aloud until Mr. McQuade's voice broke into her musings. "You have Ol' Weed 'Em Out Wyatt?"

Charlotte's eyes widened in surprise at hearing her professor's nickname. He was known around campus for his ability to help rid the college of all but the most dedicated scholars. "You know him?"

"Sure."

He waited for Charlotte to motion in the direction she'd parked her car. Now that she saw the parking lot, empty but for a few cars, and dark except where the weak street lights illuminated tiny pools of brightness, she was glad Mr. McQuade had ignored her protests about needing an escort.

"I had professor Wyatt when I went to William and Mary. He's tough." Charlotte nodded her agreement. "But fair." She decided to reserve judgment on that. "I'll tell you one thing though. He won't let you leave his class early."

Charlotte decided voicing the unladylike oath that surfaced in her mind wouldn't be a good idea. Instead, as they reached her dull blue Volvo, she searched in her purse for her keys, and admitted defeat. She'd have to tell him Friday wouldn't suit. "I'm afraid I can't make—"

"What time's your class over?"

"Four forty, but—"

"I'll meet you then."

Was he overly dedicated, or just out of his mind? High school let out at two, teachers certainly didn't have to stay past two thirty, and he was willing to wait around an extra two hours and ten minutes—and on a Friday night yet. His wife probably wanted him home early for the weekend. Charlotte glanced at the ringless hand that rested on the roof of her car. So maybe he wasn't married. Still, even if he were single, a man like this must have a lady friend, most likely lots of them.

Charlotte unlocked the car door. "I can't ask you to schedule our conference for then."

"You didn't." He gave her that heart-stopping dimpled grin and added, "I volunteered."

The car door thudded closed and Charlotte rolled down the window to continue her protest but one look at his face told her it would be futile. All right, if he wanted to waste his Friday evening, that was his business. She certainly didn't have anything better to do. Besides, the sooner she could get Elizabeth's grades straightened out, the better.

She fiddled through her keys, found the right one and jammed it into the ignition. Before she turned it, Charlotte realized what it was that had been bothering her, besides the man himself that is, since he'd begun talking to her.

"Mr. McQuade?"

"Yes." He leaned his arms on the door, his face slightly inside the open window, close to hers.

"How did you know I was Elizabeth's mother?"

He chuckled, a deep, rich sound, and reached into the car to touch a curl resting against Charlotte's cheek. "With the same glorious red hair, you had to be related."

Charlotte was certain her face was now every bit as red as her hair. Glorious, had he called it? Funny, she'd never thought of it in that way. Wild, bright, and unruly is how she'd describe it. It was a dark carrot color and curly. So curly that it resisted any attempts by her to force it into an acceptable style. Hadn't she tried all those years she'd been married to Brian to make it behave, all to no avail?

Mr. McQuade was right about one thing. Elizabeth had been gifted by her mother with the very same red hair. Charlotte could still remember the moment she first saw her daughter. Her face was wrinkled and blotchy from the birth trauma and Charlotte had thought she'd never seen anything so beautiful. Then she'd noticed the damp red ringlets that clung to her head and tears had blurred her vision. It would have been much better if she had inherited Brian's controllable straight blond hair, Charlotte remembered thinking. But the fates had decreed otherwise. "We're a pair, you and I," Charlotte had whispered to the tiny infant who clutched her finger. "A pair of curly redheads."

Charlotte fought back the memories and turned the key. The engine sputtered, coughed, and then died. Without glancing up at the man she knew still watched her, Charlotte tried again. This time, thankfully, the motor started.

"Thanks for seeing me to my car. I'll be here Friday." Charlotte looked around as she rolled up the window.

"It's a date." The words drifted in the partially closed window as Charlotte put the car into gear and started for the parking lot entrance.

A date? Charlotte's eyes flew to the rearview mirror and saw Mr. McQuade standing where she'd left him. A breeze played in the dark brown waves of his hair and caught the tail of his fish tie sending it floating over his broad shoulder. The sight made her smile. Of course he hadn't meant a date like—well, a *date*. They'd agreed to meet at a specific time to discuss a specified topic—Elizabeth.

Charlotte shook her head. She was acting like a silly teenager again. And that wasn't like her. She couldn't remember acting like this, even when she *was* a teenager. It was being back in a high school, Charlotte tried to tell herself, but even as she did, the truth forced itself to the forefront of her mind.

It was Mr. McQuade. Had she developed a crush

on him after sitting in his class for less than half an hour? The thought made her laugh aloud. She and Elizabeth couldn't have a crush on the same man. At least she couldn't fault her daughter's taste, though she was a little surprised. Mr. McQuade, whose age Charlotte imagined to be between thirty-five and forty—though certainly a well preserved forty—differed favorably from the baby faced heart throbs Elizabeth usually seemed to prefer. The object of Charlotte's own high school infatuation had been quite different.

Morris Langston. Charlotte hadn't thought of him in years. His first and last year of teaching at the rural Virginia school had been Charlotte's sophomore year. He'd been tall and skinny, with a distinctive nose and an Adam's apple that bobbed every time he swallowed. My, how that motion had fascinated her.

Well, Elizabeth could indulge in her harmless adolescent puppy love, but Charlotte would certainly take no part in it.

Charlotte turned off Richmond Road, following the quiet tree-lined street to her house. Elizabeth had left the front light on, and the cheery red door shone like a welcoming beacon. It had taken most of the summer to paint the house a pristine white, one small-paned window at a time, but Charlotte thought the work well worth it.

"That you, Mom?" Elizabeth called from the kitchen as Charlotte let herself into the cozy hall.

"Who else would it be?" Charlotte dropped her pocketbook on the hall table and leafed through the mail that Elizabeth had tossed there. Her name peeked at her through several envelope windows. Bills. Then she noticed the thick packet with her mother's

Everettsville address in the top left corner. No need to guess what that contained.

Her mother had been almost violently opposed to Charlotte's divorce. Even when Charlotte had swallowed her pride and told her mother of Brian's infidelities, her mother had excused him without batting an eye. "That's the way of men, Charlotte. You have to take the bad with the good." Apparently Brian being a doctor from a prominent family was enough good for her mother to overlook anything. But it wasn't for Charlotte.

Charlotte dropped the letter back on the table amid the scatter of bills. She'd face them all tomorrow.

"My mom's home, Ali. I better go. See you in school tomorrow." There was a pause, followed by a giggle as Charlotte walked into the kitchen. "Okay, I will. Bye." Elizabeth twisted on the counter stool and hung the receiver on its wall base. "That was Allison."

"So I gathered." Charlotte poured herself a glass of milk from the carton on the counter, wondering how long it had been out of the refrigerator.

"She called me."

"Does that mean your homework isn't finished?" The "no telephone calls till the homework is complete rule" had been initiated when the first Ds started trickling home at the beginning of the semester.

"Almost." Elizabeth slid off the vinyl seat. "I'll go do it now."

Charlotte watched as her daughter's lithe figure, so like her own, beat a hasty retreat. "I spoke with several of your teachers." The exit stopped.

"What'd they say?" Apparently Charlotte's expression carried enough meaning. "Okay, okay, I don't want to know. But, Mom, weren't they gross? Nothing like the teachers at Boswell."

At the mention of the private school Elizabeth had been forced to give up when they moved to Williamsburg, Charlotte felt her stomach muscles tighten. Then a vision of broad shoulders and dimples entered her head. She took a quick swallow from her glass to try to dispel it. "Some of them didn't seem that bad."

"You saw Mr. McQuade!"

Charlotte almost choked on her milk. It was as if Elizabeth could read her mind.

"Isn't he great!"

Charlotte reached for a napkin, remembered she'd forgotten to buy them, and got a paper towel instead. "Yes, he seems very nice."

"Nice? Mom, he's fantastic." A sudden thought seemed to hit Elizabeth. "Did he have on the tie?"

"Lizzy, I don't think you should bet with teachers about your grades."

"Oh, he didn't mind," Elizabeth answered with a wave of her hand. "So he wore it. I knew he would. Allison had her doubts, but not me." As if remembering that the topic of Allison was probably one she shouldn't bring up, Elizabeth rushed on. "Well, I bet *he* didn't have anything bad to say about my grades."

"That's one bet you may lose. I'll let you know Friday—after our conference."

"You're seeing Mr. McQuade on Friday? This Friday?"

Charlotte dried the glass she'd just washed and

nodded, noting the apprehension in her daughter's voice. Maybe things were worse than she'd thought.

"What are you going to wear?"

"What?" Charlotte turned to study Elizabeth. Where was the concern over what Mr. McQuade might say?

"I've been thinking," Elizabeth went on, ignoring her mother's question. "You should buy some new clothes. Now I know there's not much money, but you let me get school clothes, and you could use some, too. After all, you don't want to look frumpy."

Frumpy? Charlotte glanced down at her simple pleated skirt and Madras plaid blouse. Did she look frumpy? Did Mr. McQuade think so? Thoroughly annoyed by the the turn her thoughts were taking, Charlotte grabbed the dishcloth and swiped it across the counter. "I have no idea what I'm wearing Friday, nor do I care. What I am interested in is what the man has to say. About your grades," Charlotte added quickly.

"Okay, Mom." Elizabeth started backing out of the kitchen. "Gee, I hope I didn't hurt your feelings— you know with that remark about your clothes."

Charlotte looked up into her daughter's apprehensive face and her anger dissolved. It wasn't Elizabeth's fault that her mother couldn't control her thoughts. "It's all right, honey. You better do that homework and then get to bed. It's late."

"Okay. There's pizza in the refrigerator if you want it. Night, Mom."

"Night, Lizzy."

Charlotte opened the refrigerator door but decided she was too tired to eat. Besides she had some homework of her own to finish. Turning off the kitchen light, she walked through the hall, studiously ignoring her mother's letter, and went into her bedroom.

Fifteen minutes later, after reading the same passage for the fourth time, she decided to give up studying for the night. Her mind just wasn't on it. It was too busy conjuring up images of a tall, ruggedly handsome man with a fish around his neck.

TWO

She was late.

Charlotte's hands tightened on the leather-wrapped steering wheel as she waited to turn across traffic into the school parking lot. Those tourists who wanted an early dinner were already swarming along Richmond Road, heading for the many restaurants that catered to them.

Charlotte checked her watch and groaned. It wasn't bad enough that Mr. McQuade had agreed to see her late on a Friday afternoon, now her tardiness abused that kindness.

She had her choice of parking places and as Charlotte jumped out of the car, she wondered if Elizabeth's teacher was still here. Not that she'd blame him if he wasn't. She'd tried calling from a pay phone—right after she'd called the garage—but could only reach the school's after hours answering machine.

Charlotte pulled on the double doors, half expecting them to be locked, and felt a tiny shiver run through her body when they weren't. It was apprehension over her tardiness—wasn't it?

Charlotte shook her head. Why had Professor Wyatt kept the class late today of all days? And then the car. Charlotte gave her over-the-hill Volvo a scathing look before entering the building.

It was easy to find Mr. McQuade's classroom, harder to force herself to timidly knock on the door. No answer. Angered by her own sigh of relief, Charlotte tried again.

Why was she so worried about seeing Mr. McQuade? Of course, there was the fact that she was late. But that hadn't been an issue this morning when she'd tried on and discarded four outfits before becoming so completely exasperated with herself that she'd pulled on the first skirt she'd tried on, disregarding the fact that it probably made her look frumpy. Nor was she thinking about Elizabeth's grades when she impetuously used her last spray of perfume.

Now, Charlotte glanced down at her beige linen skirt, and brushed at a streak of grease. She'd probably gotten that while peering under the hood of the car. So much for making a good impression. Well, it didn't matter because her second knock went unanswered, too.

She'd just have to call him and apologize, hoping he'd give her another appointment before the term was over. Charlotte turned to walk away, then stopped. She'd leave a note, just in case she couldn't reach him at home. That way he'd be sure to know she hadn't just forgotten about their meeting.

Charlotte opened the door, her eyes widening at what she saw. Mr. McQuade hadn't gone home. He was at his desk, sound asleep. He obviously hadn't planned on this little nap, that is, if his position was any indication. His chair, poised on only two legs, leaned away from the desk at an awkward angle. By the looks of things, his feet, resting on the desk top, were all that kept his long frame balanced.

"Mr. McQuade." Charlotte whispered his name, not surprised when he didn't respond. She crept closer, uncomfortable with the prickly feeling of intimacy she experienced.

His head was bent forward, his long, dark lashes forming curved crescents beneath his closed eyes. A days' growth of whiskers shadowed the lower half of his face, and Charlotte decided he must have shaved before she'd seen him at the back to school night. Against her better judgment, Charlotte allowed her eyes to stray lower. He had loosened the knot of his tie—no fish today—and unbuttoned the top of his blue shirt, allowing her a peek at the curly brown hair that probably covered his chest. Charlotte's mouth went dry as her gaze continued the survey. His shoulders were as broad as she remembered, his stomach as flat. When she caught herself looking below the belt, Charlotte decided it was time to wake him up.

But how?

Any sudden noise or movement might tip the delicate balance of his perch, sending him sprawling onto the floor. Certainly *that* would prove a disastrous beginning to their meeting—not to mention a painful ending to his nap.

"Mr. McQuade." Charlotte was close enough now to catch the clean scent of his soap. His shirt sleeves were folded up, revealing muscled forearms, tanned by the summer sun. Cautiously, careful not to startle him, Charlotte touched his hair-roughened arm with her finger tips.

"What the . . . !"

Mac McQuade jolted awake, the nightmare from his past still fresh in his head. He grabbed onto something soft and warm, sweet smelling, as he fought to regain reality. Those eyes. He focused his own and looked into startled blue eyes filled with shock and concern. His gaze broadened and his mind registered flawless, porcelain-white skin haloed by bright red curls. Pleasure seeped through him, forcing away the last remnants of his dream, and a smile spread across his face.

"Well, it's Mrs. Handley—at last."

Charlotte could only stare in shocked silence. What had ever made her think he was in danger of falling onto the floor? The instant she'd touched him, his feet had descended to anchor his body, the chair had magically righted itself, and she'd been grabbed and hauled onto his lap. She was still there.

"You're late."

He stated this in such a matter-of-fact way that Charlotte felt compelled to explain. "And then the car wouldn't start." She'd finished the part about Professor Wyatt and was beginning on her experience with her Volvo when he interrupted.

"You need a new battery."

"That's what the man from the garage said. He jump started it but—my goodness!" Charlotte sprang to her feet. She'd been sitting on his lap, resting her hands against the solid strength of his chest while his arms surrounded her hips.

"What's wrong?" Mac's grin now spread from ear to ear. It was obvious by the rosy hue staining her cheeks that Mrs. Handley blushed easily. She had jumped off his lap like all the hounds of hell were on her heels. Too bad, because he'd kind of liked the feel of her sitting there.

What's wrong? Charlotte backed up till the desk separated them. She had actually been sitting on the lap of Elizabeth's teacher. Not that she'd had any choice. He'd awakened with such a start and pounced on her so quickly, she'd had no chance to move away. But he hadn't forced her to stay!

Charlotte straightened her purse strap and glanced up. There had been something oddly vulnerable in his eyes in that moment when he'd awakened, something that had pulled at her heart. It certainly wasn't there now. The blue-green depths of his eyes sparkled with mirth, and Charlotte couldn't help the irritation she felt, knowing she was the cause.

Well, she wouldn't have it. Maybe he did make her feel like a tongue-tied teenager, but she wasn't. She knew how to talk to people. Brian's position had required her to meet influential people. She'd once been forced to make small talk with the governor, and despite Brian's dire predictions, she'd done fine. At least the governor had appeared to enjoy himself. Charlotte cleared her throat, striving to make her voice sound calm. If Mr. McQuade could ignore that he'd pulled her onto his lap, so could she. "You wished to speak with me about Elizabeth."

"That's right. Have a seat."

He motioned her toward a student's desk and Charlotte slid into it, squirming to get comfortable, careful to keep her skirt pulled down. It was hard to feel like an adult sitting in something built for a fourteen year old, especially when the person she was talking to sat behind an impressive oak desk.

Mac buttoned his shirt, tightened his tie, and searched through the clutter in his drawer. "Here's Elizabeth's file." He held up a tan folder as he pushed his chair back. With his other hand Mac scooped up some papers that littered the floor. "I must have fallen asleep while reading these." He tossed them on the desk.

"What are they?" Charlotte remembered them being on his lap when she'd entered the room. They'd probably fallen to the floor when he'd jerked awake.

"Tenth grade creative writing exercises."

"Oh." Charlotte watched as he moved around the desk toward her. She liked it better with the massive thing forming a barrier between them. "They must be pretty boring if they put you to sleep."

"Sometimes." He winked at her conspiratorially. "Though not always, and that's when teaching seems worthwhile."

Charlotte cleared her throat again. He'd pulled another student desk to within inches of hers. "You like teaching, I gather." Did her voice sound strained?

"Sometimes." He grinned at her. "Though not always."

Charlotte felt her knees go weak and her throat tighten. The governor didn't have dimples. There could be no other logical explanation for the way she felt.

"I've spoken with your daughter's teachers," Mac began after sitting down, "and several of them are concerned about her grades."

"So am I."

Mac opened the folder. "Her records indicate she had almost straight As last year. I see an occasional B in math."

Charlotte nodded agreement. Elizabeth had never been crazy about numbers.

"She went to Boswell?"

"Yes," Charlotte agreed. "It's a private girl's school in Richmond."

"Exclusive."

Charlotte looked up, surprised that he would call it that.

"Elizabeth's word, not mine." He grinned again. The dimples deepened.

"Expensive, anyway," Charlotte laughed. With very little difficulty, she could conjure up an image of her daughter telling Mr. McQuade about her school using her best imitation of haughty grandeur. Charlottte was thankful that for all Brian's efforts, he had not turned their daughter into a snob. Elizabeth had loved Boswell because of her friends and for what the school could offer her, but she'd never been impressed because it was "the place to go."

"She didn't want to leave?"

Charlotte wasn't certain if he was asking or telling her this. Anyone who talked to Elizabeth for more than five minutes, which this man obviously had done, knew her feelings about leaving Boswell. "No, she didn't."

"A lot of kids change schools. People relocate all the time. Heck, sometimes you don't even have to move a muscle—the boundaries shift."

"I know that." What did he think she was, stupid? He acted as if she were using the move as an excuse. He's the one who brought it up. So what if she did think it was the reason? Not the only one, of course. There had been a lot of changes for Elizabeth. For Charlotte, too. But Charlotte was an adult, and she had made the decisions that had brought about all the changes.

Charlotte had tried maintaining the status quo—as much as she had been able. After she'd found out about Brian's other woman, she and Elizabeth had stayed in the large Tudor house in the right part of town. Brian had moved out. Even after the divorce, she'd tried to go on as if nothing had happened— keeping the same friends, Brian's friends, living the same lifestyle.

But it hadn't worked. It was almost as if they were still married. Oh, there hadn't been any sex. Of course, there hadn't been much of that before. That was one of the many things Brian had found lacking about her. The innocence and unsophisticated virginity he'd claimed to adore before they were married, soon became what he'd referred to as Charlotte's frigidity.

Yet even without a marriage license to bind them, Brian had continued to tell her what to do. He'd made fun of her dreams and undermined her self-confidence with his verbal abuse, till Charlotte could stand it no longer.

So Charlotte had uprooted herself and Elizabeth, moving them to Williamsburg.

Mac thrust his long legs out from under the desk. Were they making these things smaller these days? He looked at the woman beside him. It was obvious she wasn't about to confide any of her concerns in him. And why should she? They were strangers—or so she thought. He didn't feel like they were though.

Elizabeth was a likable, trusting kid who had told him all about her background—and her mother—the first time he'd met with her as her advisor. There had been occasions during that interview when Mac had known he should stop her. Personal involvement with the students and their families was not really his job. But he hadn't been able to. Elizabeth had seemed to need to talk to someone, and for some reason, he'd wanted to know about her background—about her mother.

Well, whether or not the bad grades were caused by the move, wasn't the issue. Mrs. Handley wasn't going to go back to her old life, and for that Mac admired her, so they needed to see what could be done here and now. Knowing Elizabeth, Mac didn't think the problem was that serious.

"How much time does Elizabeth spend on homework?"

"What?" Charlotte had been so deep in thought, the question took her by surprise. "Homework? Well, I'm not certain, Mr. McQuade. She's supposed to do it till she's finished, so it varies." Charlotte sighed. "But I know there's a lot of time when she's in her room, supposedly studying, that she's not. It's become quite an issue.''

"Homework has a way of doing that." Mac shifted in the too-small desk. "I have a suggestion that will probably work with Elizabeth. It should eliminate your role as enforcer, anyway."

"Enforcer?" Charlotte looked at Mr. McQuade and caught the telltale twinkle in his eye. She raised her hand when he started to speak. "No, don't tell me. Elizabeth's word, right?"

He gave her a sheepish grin. "Your daughter has an extensive vocabulary."

Charlotte surrendered to the urge and laughed. It felt amazingly good to be discussing Elizabeth with someone who didn't seem about to tell her what an awful mistake she'd made. "I'd ask you what else she said, but somehow, I don't think I want to know."

"She had only good things to say about you."

Charlotte held his gaze for a moment before she turned away, realizing how much his steady blue-green stare affected her. "What is this magic cure you have for homework?"

Now Mac laughed. "It's hardly that. I just get with the student and we come up with a contract. After it's signed, it's the student's responsibility to live up to their end of the deal."

"It sounds simple." Charlotte cocked her head.

"It is."

"Too simple."

"Haven't you ever heard the old adage 'make things as simple as possible'?"

Charlotte may have heard it, but that didn't mean she believed it. Nothing in her life had ever followed that rule. Suddenly she wished it would, so much so, that she was willing to give it a try. "Okay, if you think it will work, when do we start?" She still sounded skeptical.

"Thanks for the vote of confidence," he replied dryly, quirking his dark brow. "We'll start Monday. Elizabeth wants to do well, so we have a real advantage. By the way, I think she might need a tutor in algebra."

"Copping out on your simplistic plan already?" Charlotte couldn't help but tease him, even though her mind was feverishly adding up the unexpected cost of a tutor.

Mac shook his head. "I can tell you're going to be trouble, Charlotte Handley. When I talked with Miss Zeller, Elizabeth's math teacher, she said there were some gaps in your daughter's knowledge of the subject. It's common enough when kids change schools. Curriculums aren't always the same."

"And you think a tutor will help?" Charlotte tried to pretend she hadn't noticed his reference to her being trouble or to his use of her first name.

"Sure. Elizabeth shouldn't need one for long. Another student would probably do fine. I can get a list from Miss Zeller, if you like."

Relieved to know the tutor wasn't going to cut into her grocery budget too severely, Charlotte nodded her agreement. "Thank you, Mr. McQuade—for everything."

There really wasn't anything else to say. The problem had been discussed, a plan of attack formulated and agreed upon. So why was she still sitting there, staring into his captivating eyes?

"I have to go." Charlotte stood up abruptly, knocking her pocketbook to the floor. In her fluster over arriving late, she'd forgotten to fasten the zipper. She remembered that now. Consequently, she wasn't surprised, only extremely annoyed, when she glanced at the floor and saw the litter of keys, papers, lipstick, and personal supplies.

"Oh, my heavens." Charlotte groaned through her teeth as she knelt beside the mess and began shoveling it into the over-size handbag.

"Let me help." Charlotte looked up to see Mr. McQuade moving around the desks.

"Thanks, but I have it." Charlotte stuffed the last piece of paper, a grocery list, into the purse and stood. Maybe Brian was right. Maybe she was inept socially. What had he said? "You can take Charlotte out of the country, but you can't take the country out of Charlotte."

"Well, thank you again, Mr. McQuade." Charlotte slipped the strap over her shoulder and offered her hand. "You've been very helpful. My daughter is fortunate to have a teacher like you." Charlotte tried to ignore the zing that shot through her body when he clasped her hand in his.

Mac looked down at their hands. His nearly enveloped hers. Besides being small and finely-boned, her hand was warm and soft. Just as he'd imagined it. He slowly raised his gaze to meet her blue eyes. "How about you, Mrs. Handley? Do you feel fortunate that I'm Elizabeth's teacher?"

Charlotte tried to slip her hand from his, but his grasp was firm. "Of course," she mumbled, trying to remember what she'd have done if the governor had held her hand too long.

"Then have dinner with me."

"What?" This time when Charlotte pulled her hand, he let it go. "Oh, dinner. I can't, really. I'm sorry, but Elizabeth . . ." She let the sentence drift off because she had no way to honestly finish it. She'd told Elizabeth to reheat the leftover lasagna for herself when Charlotte had called her from the same pay phone she'd used to contact the garage and school. But just because her daughter wasn't waiting at home with her beak open like a hungry baby bird, didn't mean Charlotte would go out to dinner with her teacher.

Besides, she was certain he'd just asked her to be polite. It was getting awfully late. The poor man was probably starved. And the way she still hung around, he must figure the only way to feed himself was to take her along.

"I understand." Mac wasn't as surprised by her answer as he was at himself for asking. He certainly hadn't planned to do it. There was just something about her he found damn near impossible to resist. He wasn't even sure what it was. Red hair had never been his thing, though he had to admit her curling mass was fascinating. Wild and crackling with fiery sparks, it formed an intriguing contrast to the quiet strength of the woman herself. Mac mentally shook himself. For Pete's sake he'd only asked her for dinner—and pizza was all he'd had in mind.

"Come on, I'll walk you to your car." He held up his hand when he sensed she was about to protest. "It's on my way."

Mac shoved a few student papers into his briefcase and turned back to find her still standing beside the desks. As he stared at her, she glanced up at him with those bluer than blue eyes, and Mac felt an uncontrollable smile tilt the corners of his mouth. Forget the hair, it was the eyes he found irresistible. He'd always been a sucker for the color blue.

As they had several nights ago, Charlotte and Mac walked down the empty hall, then through the door to the equally empty parking lot. Mac wondered if they were forming some sort of pattern for their relationship. Then he remembered they didn't have a relationship.

"My car's right over there." Charlotte pointed out the Volvo that she was certain he remembered from the other night. Even if he hadn't, he'd have known because it was one of only two cars on the lot. The other was a dark green Jeep with its top down. Charlotte assumed it was his and decided the rugged, outdoorsy automobile suited him.

A chill that had been held at bay by the bright autumn sun now frosted the grainy twilight. Charlotte hurried across the parking lot, rubbing her arms in an attempt to ward off the goose bumps.

"Cold?"

Before Charlotte could respond to his question, she felt the welcome warmth of Mr. McQuade's sports jacket envelope her small frame. She started to protest, but when she looked at him he smiled, and they *were* close to her car. Besides, the jacket smelled so wonderfully like him.

But she did take it off before sliding into the

driver's seat, handing it back to him with a thank you.

The last time she'd been in this position, with Mr. McQuade standing beside her car, the Volvo had started, albeit reluctantly. Charlotte should have known her luck wouldn't hold. Twice she turned the key. Twice the engine teased her with a hopeful growl, only to die a slow choking death. The third time it simply ground itself out, weakly.

Charlotte's foot ached to kick at the pedals, the floor board, the whole rotten car. Why did this have to happen now? She knew she needed a new battery and she was going to get one tomorrow. Charlotte could almost hear Brian telling her how ill prepared to deal with problems she was. Naive, he had called her. And incompetent.

Well, maybe she had a lot to learn, but she intended to do it. She was happy making decisions for herself, following her own advice, even making her own mistakes. She just wished Elizabeth's teacher wasn't standing there, watching her.

Charlotte opened the car door. "You really don't have to stay with me," she said, searching in her wallet for another quarter. "I'll just call the garage. They were very prompt earlier." She started toward the outside phone by the school door, hoping Mr. McQuade would take the hint and leave.

He didn't.

"I have jumper cables."

"Please, don't go to any bother," Charlotte turned to tell him, but he was already jogging toward his Jeep. "I really can handle this myself." Fine words, but he didn't hear them. How could he, when he'd already stuck his head under her hood?

Ten minutes later her traitorous car was humming along the pike. Charlotte had been adamant about her refusal to let him take her to get a new battery. She didn't need another man to take care of her, especially a man who made her pulse speed up whenever she saw him.

No, she would do fine on her own. Mr. McQuade was not someone she needed—or wanted.

THREE

The stirring strains of a Sousa march drifted down Duke of Gloucester Street. Charlotte, using her hand to shade her squinted eyes against the morning sun, looked past the quaint, eighteenth century shops and houses toward the Wren Building at the far end of the road.

"Can you see anything?"

Charlotte glanced over at her daughter's eager face. "Not yet. But it won't be long now."

Elizabeth let an exaggerated sigh escape her lips, seemingly resigned to waiting a little longer while Charlotte experienced a sudden pang of deja vu. Had it really been ten years ago that Charlotte stood on Broad Street in Richmond, a bundled up Elizabeth clutching her hand, squealing, "Mommy, Mommy, is the band coming?"

"Look!"

Jerked from her memories by Elizabeth's excited voice, Charlotte stared in the direction from which the Homecoming parade was to come.

"Not there, Mom. There!" Elizabeth's finger arrowed to a spot across the cobblestoned street, directly in front of Chowning's Tavern.

"Elizabeth, it is not polite to . . . point." The end of her reprimand mumbled to a near whisper as Charlotte noticed the reason for her daughter's elation: Mr. McQuade.

Not that Charlotte was surprised he was here. This *was* William and Mary's Homecoming, and hadn't he told her he'd attended the college? Besides, Charlotte had seen him earlier. Her gaze had been drawn to his tall, athletic form as she and Elizabeth had wended their way through the crowds standing on the brick pavements. But she certainly hadn't drawn attention to herself, especially when she'd noticed he was talking to a sleek, slender blonde. And when Elizabeth had suggested a spot further down the street to watch the parade, Charlotte had been thankful that Mr. McQuade hadn't seen her.

Of course, *she* hadn't been practically standing on her head like the fourteen year old at her side was now doing. "Elizabeth." The word hissed through Charlotte's teeth. "Would you stop waving your arms, you'll . . . you'll miss the parade." Even Charlotte realized the foolishness of her words since the band was still at least two blocks down the street.

Besides, it was too late. Mr. McQuade's hand lifted in a friendly salute as he stepped off the curb, heading their way.

"He's coming over here, Mom!"

Charlotte didn't say anything, she couldn't. Just watching him walk toward her was doing strange things to Charlotte's insides. Her throat tightened, butterflies invaded her stomach, and she could only be thankful that no one was listening to her heart with a stethoscope.

He wore his well-worn jeans—well, and Charlotte was reminded of the advertising slogan "shrink to fit." The soft denim molded the strong muscles of his thighs, his narrow waist, and—elsewhere. Blood rushed to Charlotte's cheeks as she realized exactly where she'd been looking.

"Great day for a parade, isn't it?" Mac almost grimaced at his line. He'd wanted to say something clever and witty, but as he'd crossed the street, he'd caught a glimpse of the sun reflecting off Charlotte Handley's hair. His mouth had gone dry. It appeared his brain had, too.

Obviously, Elizabeth didn't notice his dilemma, for she bubbled on about how exciting the day was, and how neat it was that she'd spotted him. Her mother, on the other hand, had given him only the slightest of nods before turning back toward the street. Apparently she wasn't going to let *this* parade pass her by.

"Don't you think so, Mom?" Charlotte heard her daughter's voice over the blare of brass instruments. The band had finally arrived. But for all the noise, Charlotte had barely noticed. Mr. McQuade had taken up position behind her, and the swell of the crowd had knocked him against her several times. He'd apologized, but that had done nothing to decharge the electric spark that had shot through her each time their bodies touched.

"Don't I think what, Lizzy?" Charlotte decided to concentrate on her daughter. After all, that's why she'd taken the day off from her studies. So she could be with Elizabeth.

"Their uniforms, aren't they great?"

Charlotte looked back at the band. "Yes, they're very . . . colorful." What else could she say about green and gold?

Following the last row of tubas came the floats. Each sorority and fraternity entered their creation, hoping to win the award for most original theme. Charlotte thought "outlandish" might have been a better term.

"That's my old frat." Mr. McQuade's breath tickled across Charlotte's cheek as he leaned forward to point out the float passing by. It sported four Ionic columns and close to a dozen young men wearing togas that looked amazingly like bedsheets.

"Animal House lives." Charlotte didn't know what made her say it, and she was half afraid Elizabeth's teacher would take offense. Brian had been very defensive about his college fraternity. But she didn't even have to glance around to know that Mr. McQuade was laughing. The deep rumbling sound vibrated through her body.

"It wasn't quite that bad—but close." Mac leaned perhaps a little nearer than necessary to Charlotte's ear. Her hair smelled as sunny clean as it looked.

He told Charlotte and Elizabeth a story about making enough tissue paper roses to cover a similar float during his senior year. The thought of tall, masculine Mr. McQuade creating dainty flowers was enough to make Charlotte laugh, and almost enough to make her forget how uncomfortable that very same masculinity made her feel.

But being around him wouldn't last much longer. Williamsburg was a small town, and William and Mary a small college. There were only so many people who could march down the street and still insure an audience. Thankfully, the parade was short.

As the drum cadence of the high school band faded, Charlotte knew a sense of relief. For whatever reason Mr. McQuade had stayed with them during the parade—and Charlotte was convinced it was Elizabeth's near insistence—he would now be free to leave. And he'd probably go back to that slinky blonde. Annoyed with her train of thought and the accompanying pang of jealousy, Charlotte turned toward him.

"Well, it was nice to see you again, Mr. McQuade." She thought about offering him her hand, but remembering the electricity from last time they'd shaken hands, decided against it. "Come on, Elizabeth, we'd better be going."

"But what about the cider?"

"The what?" Charlotte had already taken several steps along the sidewalk when she turned to look at her daughter. Elizabeth hadn't moved.

"Cider! Mom, you said we could get cider and gingerbread men at Chownings. Don't you remember?"

Charlotte did recall the plan, but of course, that had been before Mr. McQuade appeared on the scene. Still, leaving him to partake of a snack was as good as leaving him to scurry home.

"Sure, I remember. Let's go." Charlotte started back toward Elizabeth and the tavern.

"Maybe Mr. McQuade would like to go, too. They have really great cookies." Elizabeth's words were almost a plea.

Charlotte stared at her daughter, wondering why she'd ever considered child abuse such a heinous crime. "Oh, I'm certain Mr. McQuade has other plans. He's—"

"No, I don't," Mac cut in before he and Elizabeth started across the street toward Chowning's Tavern. Charlotte could do nothing but follow, especially when he turned and extended his hand. She didn't take it, but she did allow him to guide her around a pile of horse droppings in the middle of the road.

"The only disadvantage I know to horse-drawn carriage rides," he remarked as his hand nudged the small of her back.

Because they chose to take their refreshments outside under the arbor, Mac, Charlotte, and Elizabeth didn't have to wait long to be seated. A young man in colonial garb, cotton stockings, and knee breeches, offered them a menu.

"We're only having something to drink," Charlotte was quick to point out.

"Are you sure you couldn't eat something more? Brunswick stew, maybe?" Mr. McQuade's blue-green eyes looked from mother to daughter.

Charlotte held her breath when she heard Elizabeth begin to answer.

"Gee, we had a really late breakfast, but if you want some lunch go ahead. We don't mind waiting, do we, Mom?"

"No, gingerbread and cider is fine." He didn't give Charlotte time to answer, but he did look at her when he added, "I like to sleep in on Saturday mornings, too."

Charlotte couldn't stop the vision that invaded her

mind of a lazy Mr. McQuade, lolling against propped pillows. His hair was sleep tossed, his aquamarine eyes sensual, and his smile satisfied.

A waitress in a mobcap brought frosty mugs of cider and warm, spicy smelling gingerbread cookies. When she placed the bill on the table, Charlotte was tempted to grab for it. If Mr. McQuade hadn't smoothly slipped it into his lap, she would have.

"There's Ali!" Elizabeth's voice sliced through the silence that accompanied the sipping of cider. "Can I go talk to her for just a minute, Mom, please?"

Charlotte chewed a molasses sweet cookie, using the time to consider her answer. Not for anything would she admit that she wanted her daughter's presence as protection against her growing awareness of Elizabeth's teacher. And what other reason could she give for refusing? "I guess so, but don't be long," she called after Elizabeth's already retreating form.

"Great kid." Mac had risen when Elizabeth jumped up, and now he settled back onto the bench beside Charlotte.

"I'm afraid she's a bit too forward."

"What do you mean?" Mac took a drink of the tangy cider, wiping his mouth with the gingham napkin.

Charlotte folded her hands on the rough-hewn table. "You really don't have to stay with us, just because she asks."

"You didn't want me to join you for cider?"

"No . . . I mean yes." Charlotte sighed then started again. She certainly didn't want to hurt his feelings. "It's only that I wouldn't want you to feel obligated."

"I don't."

There was that heart-stopping smile again, complete with dimples. Charlotte forced herself not to look down at her hands. "I want to thank you, Mr. McQuade, for getting Elizabeth the list of tutors."

"You're welcome. Did she find one? And it's Mac." At her questioning expression, he added, "My name. It's Mac."

"Oh." Hesitating only a moment, she informed, "Mine's Charlotte."

"Yes, I know."

Of course he did. Hadn't he called her that the last time she'd seen him? Steering the conversation back to less personal ground, Charlotte said, "Todd Park's her tutor."

"I know Todd. He was in my creative writing class last year. Nice kid. He's on the football team, too, if I remember correctly."

"You do. I think Elizabeth is more impressed with that and his blue eyes than with his knowledge of algebra."

"Blue eyes are easy to get hung up on."

His tone was so easy going that for a moment Charlotte forgot *she* had blue eyes or that he was staring into them. She looked away, breaking the hypnotic pull of his sea-green gaze.

"The homework contract works, too." Charlotte did have a lot to thank him for. There had been little or no conflict last week about settling down to study—the phone hadn't even been an issue. And the algebra test Elizabeth had brought home on Thursday had a red C scrawled across the top. Not terrific, but certainly better than the Ds she had been getting. Charlotte had just decided to tell him about the grade when she heard Elizabeth calling.

"Mom!" Elizabeth leaned over the fence that separated Chowning's outdoor tables from the village green. "Ali's going to the game, too."

"Hi, Mrs. Handley." Allison Davis, Elizabeth's best friend, was dressed in her high school band uniform. She gave Charlotte a braces-laced smile. It grew wider, if perhaps a little disbelieving, when she looked to Charlotte's right. "How are you, Mr. McQuade?"

"I'm fine, Allison. The band sounded great!"

"We've been practicing a lot." The laugh that accompanied Ali's statement wasn't quite a giggle, but close.

"Is it okay if I walk over to Cary Field with Ali? I could save you a seat," Elizabeth pointed out. "Would you hand me my cookie, please?"

Wordlessly, Charlotte picked up the gingerbread boy and passed it to Elizabeth. The day had started out to be so simple, but somehow along the way, she'd lost control. Charlotte had a sneaking suspicion it had happened when Elizabeth spotted her teacher.

"Are you going to the football game?"

Charlotte stopped worrying about what answer to give Elizabeth and looked over at Mr. McQuade. "Well, yes I was. . . ."

"Me, too. You have end zone tickets?"

Charlotte nodded.

"Great!"

Yeah, great. Ten minutes later Charlotte crunched along with Mac McQuade through fallen leaves. They were taking a wooded path—a short-cut he knew—

toward the football stadium. Elizabeth and Ali were long gone. They'd run off the moment Charlotte had given her reluctant endorsement to their plan. What choice did she have? She could hardly tell her daughter that she had to stay because her mother didn't want to be alone with Mr. McQuade. Especially since the truth was she did want to be with him.

He really was a nice man, kind and considerate, and except for the distracting physical attraction she felt, Charlotte enjoyed his company. It wasn't his fault that she couldn't control her lusty thoughts, anymore than he could help it that he was so overwhelmingly masculine.

"Are you uncomfortable with me?"

Charlotte was jerked from her musings by his words. Her jaw dropped. Was he a mind reader, too? "Of course not . . ." she stuttered. "Why should I be?"

"I'm not sure." He shrugged his broad shoulders. "I just get the feeling you are."

"Well, I'm not," Charlotte lied.

"Good." Sun filtered through the bare branches overhead, touching Charlotte's hair, setting it aflame. The sight made Mac smile. "I was afraid you might have some objection to me because I'm Elizabeth's teacher. This isn't the eighteenth century, and I'm hardly some maiden schoolmarm."

He certainly didn't have to tell her *that!* But though Charlotte made some comment to show her agreement, part of her wasn't certain his position didn't have something to do with her unease. Divorced women didn't go out with their children's teachers. Did they? But, she reminded herself, this wasn't a date. They'd just happened upon each other, thanks to Elizabeth.

Besides, Charlotte wasn't interested in any man. Gaining her freedom from Brian had been too hard. Now she wanted to prove to herself that she could take care of Elizabeth—and herself. Still, there was no reason they couldn't be friends. But friends knew things about each other, and she knew very little about this man, except that he was a good teacher and seemed to be great with kids.

"Do you have children of your own, Mr . . . Mac?" Charlotte didn't realize she'd voiced the question that had been playing around in her head till he answered.

"No, I'm not married."

"Oh." Was that what she'd really wanted to know?

"I was, once. She divorced me shortly after I got back from 'Nam."

"I'm sorry." Charlotte felt a sudden sharp stab of dislike for any woman that would leave a man like Mac, especially after he'd been to war.

"That's okay. It was a long time ago. And it was probably for the best."

Wondering what he meant by that, Charlotte let him take her hand to guide her through the crowd milling around the ticket booth at the stadium. Instantaneously, her heart started beating faster and her knees weakened. Could she be pals with a man that made her feel this way?

"How about you?"

"Me?" Charlotte remembered they had been discussing marital status. "Oh, Elizabeth's father and I are divorced."

"I know." He pulled her through the gate. "How long ago?"

"About a year and a half." Charlotte wasn't sure she wanted to be discussing this with her daughter's teacher, but then she had brought up the subject.

"Mom! Mr. McQuade! Up here!"

Charlotte looked up gratefully at Elizabeth's waving arms, then followed Mac up the bleachers toward the seats her daughter had saved. He still held her hand. Charlotte wondered if Elizabeth noticed.

"What kept you two so long? I was afraid the game would start before you got here."

Mac turned and winked at the girls sitting behind him. "Hey, when you get as old as I am, we'll see if you go running around quite so fast."

"Oh, you're not old, Mr. McQuade." Charlotte felt the jab her daughter gave Mac's arm through their linked hands. "Besides, I happen to know you're sponsor of the jogging club."

Mac's laughter gave Charlotte the opportunity to slip her hand from his. Folding hers in her lap didn't help the sudden lack of warmth she experienced.

Charlotte had always been certain she didn't like football. Too boring, she'd frequently told herself. And so complicated. She'd only agreed to come to the Homecoming game because Elizabeth had practically begged. That's why the enjoyment she experienced seemed so surprising. For someone who didn't know the difference between a quarterback sneak and a first down, Charlotte found the play extraordinarily easy to follow.

Of course, the explanation was simple. Mac McQuade. He unscrambled the mysteries of the game so naturally that Charlotte never felt ignorant. Her questions were not laughed at, nor was her awakening interest ridiculed. She sat beside him, conscious of every time his jeans-clad thigh brushed hers, wondering how she could have ever thought football dull.

So why then did she grasp at an excuse to reject his offer to walk her and Elizabeth home after the Indians had won the game?

"We had planned on staying in town to do some shopping." Charlotte tried to ignore the look of surprise that shot across Elizabeth's face. "But thank you very much. We had a wonderful time. Didn't we, Lizzy?"

"So what are we shopping for?"

Charlotte had been watching Mac move away from them through the few, lingering football fans. The day had grown warm and he'd removed his fisherman knit sweater, carelessly slinging it across his broad shoulder.

"Shopping." What *was* she to go shopping for? That was the problem with telling a little white lie in front of her daughter. "I thought I might look at some clothes. You said—"

"Clothes! That's great, Mom."

Twenty minutes later Charlotte stood in a small boutique in Merchant's Square. The block of shops and restaurants offered modern shopping with eighteenth century charm.

"Well, are you going to try that on?"

Charlotte shook her head. "No, I don't think so."

"Gee, you stared at it so long, I thought you really liked it."

Charlotte looked down at the dress she held, actually seeing it for the first time. It was an obnoxious color, not to mention the wrong size. She hung it back on the rack. "I don't see anything I want. Maybe we should go on home."

"Mo-o-o-m! We just got here. Besides, there are some really neat things over here." Elizabeth led the way.

For the next two hours, till the shops closed their doors for another day, Elizabeth led the way. Charlotte tried on clothes until she thought she'd be perfectly happy if everyone wore burlap sacks.

When they finally made their way home, Charlotte was tired but happy. The shopping trip had given her an opportunity to spend time with Elizabeth—and it had taken her mind off Mac McQuade.

The phone was ringing as Charlotte unlocked the front door. She dropped her pocketbook and her one purchase, an outrageously expensive scarf that Elizabeth said would update her blue wool dress, on the hall table.

"Hello." Charlotte's breathing came in raspy gulps as she pulled the receiver from its wall bracket. Running into the kitchen, she'd had the wildest thought that it might be Mac McQuade calling her. That wasn't why she'd hurried, of course, but it might have something to do with the rapid pounding of her heart. She wasn't *that* out of shape! "Charlotte, is that you?" The voice on the other end of the connection shrieked into Charlotte's ear.

"Hi, Mom. Yes, it's me." Charlotte slumped onto the kitchen stool. What had ever made her think Mac would call her? It hadn't been three hours ago that she'd seen him. And though she'd been the one to cut their afternoon short, he certainly hadn't raised much of a fuss.

"You sound funny, Charlotte honey."

Charlotte's hand fluttered to her throat, and she worked to calm her breathing. "I was running. Elizabeth and I just got home."

"And don't I know it. I've been trying to call you all afternoon. Mary Ellen said not to worry, but you know me. I just kept imagining all sorts of things that could have happened to you, being alone like you are."

Charlotte felt her blood pressure rising. "I'm not alone, Mom. Elizabeth and I—"

"Where've you been, honey?"

"We went to a football game, then shopping. How's Mary Ellen . . . and Jim?" Charlotte hoped asking about her sister and brother-in-law might give her mother something else to talk about.

"They're fine. The kids, too, though Young Jim fell out of a tree and busted up his arm."

Charlotte's expression of concern was lost on her mother.

"You say you were shopping. Do you have the money for that now, Charlotte? Things are a lot different since Brian isn't around."

Charlotte silently counted to ten. "I'm doing just fine, Mother. Elizabeth and I both are."

"It's been a long time since I've seen her. Have you decided if you can come home for Thanksgiving yet? You did get my letter, didn't you?"

"Yes, I got it. *My* letter should reach you the beginning of next week."

"Well, what about Thanksgiving? I'll be all alone, you know. Mary Ellen's going down to Jim's momma's. She's been real poorly lately."

Charlotte drew a deep breath. "I suggested in my letter that you come here."

"Oh, now Charlotte."

"You'd like Williamsburg, Mom. And besides, you never visit us." Charlotte didn't mention that Brian had never made any effort to make her family feel welcome.

"Well, I don't know . . . "

"Mary Ellen and Jim could drive you to the bus depot in Danville, and I'd pick you up here." When Charlotte didn't hear anything but silence coming through the wire, she added, "You think about it, and I'll call you next week."

The rest of the conversation centered around residents of Everettsville, most of whom Charlotte remembered from the years she'd spent in the small town. Everettsville was not the kind of town people tended to leave. Of course, Charlotte had. But she'd been an exception.

She'd been the first member of her family to go away to college, and on scholarship, yet. She'd been so proud—and so green. Charlotte had thought nothing could stand in the way of getting her degree.

That was before she met Brian Handley. Polished, worldly, and slick as a greased pig, he'd convinced her that the only important thing for Charlotte was to be his wife.

"Good-bye now, Charlotte. I worry about you." Her mother's voice, full of concern, brought Charlotte back to the present.

"I know you do, but it really isn't necessary. I'm a grown woman and I can . . . Mom?" It took Charlotte a moment to realize she was explaining to a dead phone.

"Is Grandmom coming for Thanksgiving?" Elizabeth walked into the room and headed straight for the refrigerator.

"I'm not sure." Charlotte hung up the phone and caught a glimpse of the cold cuts Elizabeth stacked on the counter. "Lizzy, you can't eat all that. You'll spoil your dinner."

"But, Mom, I'm hungry! Besides, it's time for dinner."

Charlotte glanced at the clock over the stove. "You're right. What do you want to eat?"

"How about sandwiches? I could fix you one, too."

Though sandwiches were not exactly what Charlotte viewed as a well-balanced meal, the thought of taking a break while her daughter fixed them was very appealing. "Okay, you've got yourself a deal. But," Charlotte gave Elizabeth's hair a playful tug, "only if you promise to put extra mayo on mine."

"Aw, Mom." Elizabeth ducked away from her mother. "Hey, do you think we could go get some ice cream later?"

"I knew there was a catch to this." Charlotte tried to scowl, but knew she failed miserably. "Okay, ice cream it is. We'll fulfill our daily requirement of dairy products."

"I like the way your mind works, Mom." Elizabeth began slicing tomatoes. "Maybe we'll run into Mr. McQuade again."

"I wouldn't count on it. And that reminds me, young lady. In the future, if we do, I would appreciate it if you wouldn't force him to stay with us." This time Charlotte's scowl was a lot more convincing.

* * *

Bottom of the ninth, two men on base, Mays at the plate. Drysdale's first pitch is a fast ball. Swing! Strike one. The crowd goes wild! Then a hush blankets the stadium as Drysdale winds up, tossing a quick glance over his shoulder to first, and delivers. It's a curve ball. No, it's . . .

With panic, I feel my memory's fragile hold on the game falter. Jungle sounds, ominous in their familiarity, penetrate, then obliterate, the cheering fans. Frantically, I try to remember. Did Drysdale throw a curve ball or slider? Slider or curve ball? But it's no use. My mind has returned to the present—to the gruesome reality of my bamboo cage. Foolishly, I grow angry—not with my captors, the jeering Viet Cong who taunt and chide me, but with myself. If only my recollections were more perfect. If only I'd paid greater attention to details when as a fourteen year old I'd watched this game, then perhaps I could live in my dream world longer. For my dream world is all that keeps me sane.

Mac McQuade stared at the words displayed on his computer screen. It had been almost a year since he'd written them; almost fifteen years since he'd lived them. He read and reread. Revising, he told himself, though he rarely changed so much as a period.

He should send the manuscript away. His agent had repeatedly asked for it. But still Mac hesitated. Sometimes he thought it was fear that forced him to hold on to it. But that was ridiculous. After what he'd experienced, nothing could ever scare him again.

With a click Mac turned off the computer, stood up and stretched his stiff muscles. It was late, nearly one o'clock, and he'd been working for hours. The beer he'd nursed through most of the evening was warm and Mac took the long-necked bottle into the kitchen and threw it away.

A quick shower, and Mac was ready for bed. He stretched out on the king-size mattress that comfortably accommodated his large frame. Even after fifteen years, he still appreciated the luxury of clean sheets and a soft bed. He was glad, too, that he no longer had to fill his thoughts with baseball trivia because right now he was having too pleasant a time thinking of something else.

Mac smiled as a vision of serene blue eyes and fiery red hair danced through his mind. Charlotte Handley. He hadn't been able to stop thinking about her since she'd walked into his classroom and stared at his tie. But though he'd be willing to bet she wasn't as oblivious to him as she pretended, she still did all she could to ignore him.

He chuckled to himself. Maybe he'd just have to wear the damn fish again.

FOUR

"Lizzy, will you get the door? If it's Sally Reinert, the book she lent me is on the hall table."

Charlotte stood on the seat of a rickety step chair trying to position a strip of wallpaper. "It's prepasted, very simple to put up," the young man at the hardware store had told her. Right now she'd love to wrap the entire roll around his scrawny neck. That would certainly erase the smug expression from his face.

Biting her bottom lip, Charlotte studied the bright red and blue calico design. She'd loved its cozy colors in the store, and only hoped she felt the same after she managed to cover her kitchen walls with it. Charlotte wiggled the sodden paper a little to the left as she heard footsteps stop at the archway leading from the tiny dining room.

"Do I have the pattern lined up at the seam, Lizzy?"

Mac McQuade stood in the doorway, smiling at the sight before him. Charlotte Handley was perched, quite precariously to his way of thinking, on a chair with her hands stretched high above her head. Ragged jeans covered her firm, little fanny and her long, dancer's legs. The bright hair that he found so intriguing was all but concealed by a large, red railroad handkerchief.

"I think it needs to come down about an eighth of an inch."

"Wha . . . ?"

Charlotte had been just about to ask her daughter what the big hold up was—her arms seemed permanently lifted toward the heavens, and she had a terrible crick in her neck—when she heard the deep, amusement-laced baritone. All thoughts of wallcoverings fled her mind as she jerked her body around.

Unfortunately, the metal chair seat was slicked with its share of the pasty liquid that ran off the back of the wallpaper. Charlotte felt her feet slip at the same time she caught a glimpse of the startled expression on Elizabeth's teacher's handsome face. She could only guess it matched her own.

Confident that the next thing she'd hit would be the hard, linoleum floor, Charlotte was shocked to find herself hauled up against something equally hard but a lot more comfortable—Mac McQuade's chest.

Her sticky hands grasped his broad shoulders, leaving wet prints on his locker room gray tee shirt.

"Did you hurt yourself?"

His expression was full of concern now. Charlotte had little difficulty observing this since her face was only inches from his. She could easily see the tiny lines radiating from his sea-green eyes and the slight indentations that marked the spots for his dimples. Noticing his slightly pugnacious nose, firm, sensual lips, and shadow of whiskers was easy; answering his question was not.

"Are you all right?" he demanded, tightening his arms that held her firmly half a foot off the floor.

"Yes," Charlotte answered, feeling far from all right. This morning, expecting to do nothing but stay at home and wallpaper the kitchen, she'd opted to go braless. Now, with her breasts pressed against Mac's muscular chest, she realized her mistake. The threadbare flannel of her shirt, gently abraded the stiff, sensitive points of her nipples. She wondered if Elizabeth's teacher could feel them.

Mac hadn't meant to scare Charlotte into falling, and once he'd caught her, he certainly hadn't meant to hold her so long. But there was no denying how good it felt. Her body's reaction to their intimate position was obvious, as was his own. What wasn't clear to him was what he planned to do about it.

Then her small, pink tongue licked her bottom lip in an unconscious, nervous way, and Mac knew he had no choice. He felt her tiny gasp of surprise as his mouth touched hers, gently at first, then more urgently. He twisted his head, seeking a better angle before his tongue thrust between her lips. The realization that she didn't deny him entrance sent his heart racing.

A kiss could make you feel like this? The question was the last conscious thought Charlotte had before her mind shut down. Her hands clutched at the crew neck of his shirt in a frantic rhythm that matched the strokes of his tongue. Hers joined the foray, responding blindly to his unvoiced invitation.

"Mom, what was that racket?"

Charlotte felt Mac's arms stiffen as he broke off the kiss and let her slide swiftly to the floor. She grabbed the chair back to keep from falling as he busied himself picking up the strip of wallpaper that had fallen unheeded in a slimy heap.

"I accidentally scared your mother and she almost fell."

Mac had obviously realized that she wouldn't or couldn't answer her daughter's question. Charlotte glanced from Elizabeth to Mac, who was still fooling with the wallpaper, his back to both of them. After having brushed against the bulging ridge on the front of his jeans when he'd lowered her to the floor, Charlotte was glad he didn't turn around. As a matter of fact, wished they could both crawl off someplace and recover their wits before they had to face Elizabeth.

"You fell?" Elizabeth sounded upset.

"No, no, Mac . . . Mr. McQuade caught me." Charlotte managed a weak smile.

"Are you sure you weren't hurt? You sound awfully funny."

"I'm . . ." Charlotte cleared her throat and started again. "I'm fine." When had Elizabeth become so perceptive? Well, at least she didn't seem to have seen the kiss. Or if she did, she wasn't letting on. Charlotte's eyes narrowed, as that thought hit her. She studied Elizabeth's guileless face. No answer there.

Turning away, Charlotte decided the best thing to

do was to act as if nothing had happened. But she hadn't counted on touching Mac's hand when she reached for the wallpaper. The contact forced her gaze to meet his. He hadn't yet been able to conceal the passion that had exploded between them. Charlotte wondered if Elizabeth had been able to read the same desire in her eyes.

"Is this piece ripped?" Charlotte tore her gaze from his and made a great display of examining the flowered paper.

"No, but I don't think it can be used."

"You're right, of course. It's a good thing I bought extra. You see I've never done anything like this before, and I thought I might make a mistake or two. The man at the hardware store suggested I hire someone, but I said no, I could do it. But I obviously need some practice." Charlotte stopped short. Did Elizabeth notice how she rambled? Did Mac McQuade?

Charlotte tried again to pull herself together. For heaven's sake, it was only a kiss. But what a kiss! Even though Charlotte had never experienced anything like it before, she knew it was the kind that led to the bedroom. She had a sudden sharp memory of the way his body felt pressed intimately to hers. Forget the bedroom. It was the kind of kiss that led to scattered clothes and wild mating on the kitchen floor.

The thought brought color to Charlotte's cheeks and determination to her mind. She had no intention of rolling around on the linoleum with her daughter's teacher. The first step was to get rid of him. What was he doing here, anyway? Before she could devise a polite way to inquire, he further complicated things by asking if he could help.

"No!"

"Yeah!"

The words were spoken almost simultaneously by Charlotte and Elizabeth, respectively.

"You must have something else you'd rather be doing." Charlotte tried to soften her abrupt negative response. After all, she didn't want to alienate the man, just get rid of him so she could concentrate on what she was doing.

"I can't think of anything." Mac leaned his hip against the butcher block kitchen table, leafing through the paperback book that touted the title *Ten Easy Steps to Wallpapering Like a Pro*. There was no doubt in his mind that she wanted him to leave, yet some perverse flaw in his character made him determined to stay.

Charlotte had tried to thwart all his attempts to help her. Only where Elizabeth's welfare was concerned did she accept his assistance. Well, he'd wanted her to notice him, and after the kiss they'd shared, he was certain she had. So now she could start getting use to having him around. Because that kiss had been as wild, red-hot, and full of fiery sparks as her hair. And it had nearly knocked his socks off. No way around it, he planned to see a lot more of Charlotte Handley.

"Have you ever hung wallpaper before?" She sounded like a personnel manager interviewing a prospective employee—one that didn't stand much chance of getting the job.

"I'd say I have about as much experience as you."

Charlotte tried to ignore his grin and concentrate on his words. She'd already told him she'd never done this before, so obviously his experience was zilch. Of course lack of expertise had never stopped Brian from taking over anything and everything she'd tried to do. One of the reasons she enjoyed working on this house was that she could make her own decisions—and mistakes—without answering to anyone. She thought of the way her ex-husband had even criticized her gardening, hiring someone so that the grounds would compliment the *House Beautiful* two-story-Tudor, made her angry all over again.

There was no way she'd let that happen to her again. She'd do the wallpaper herself, dammit. And if she needed help, there was Lizzy. Lizzy, who was now taking a soda out of the refrigerator for herself. She'd already given one to her teacher.

"You want one, Mom?"

"No." Okay, she'd give him till he finished his drink. Then he'd have to go. Besides she could use a little break. Charlotte let her neck fall back and rolled her shoulders, trying to relieve their stiffness.

"Sore?" The word sounded almost like a caress, and Charlotte looked at Mac, realizing what she was doing and how it must look to him. She resisted the urge to fold her arms across her breasts as she shook her head. From now on she'd be sure to wear a bra.

Mac's hearty gulp of cola burned its way down his throat to his stomach. He was trying to put that kiss out of his mind, but seeing Charlotte Handley's chest outlined in faded plaid wasn't helping any. It was a good thing Elizabeth lounged against the counter or he might be tempted to take up where they'd left off.

"Good choice." Mac examined an unopened roll of wallpaper. "Your kitchen will look old-fashioned and cozy when you get it up."

"Do you really think so?" That was exactly what Charlotte had thought. The paper reminded her of the curtains in the bedroom where she'd grown up, bright, cheery, and a little bit country.

"Sure. So, what do you want me to do?" Mac crushed the aluminum can and tossed it into the trash basket.

What did she want him to do? She wanted him to leave. To go back to doing whatever it was he did on Saturdays, besides sleeping late. Darn, why did she have to remember he'd told her that?

It seemed as if she wasn't going to get her wish, because he looked at her expectantly, awaiting her orders. At least he wasn't telling *her* what to do. But she knew men. That would come later.

But it didn't. At least not while they covered the wall around the cupboards and back door. By the time they broke for lunch, the kitchen was starting to take on a new character. The three of them had measured, pasted, and papered and never once had Mac given Charlotte an order. Oh, he'd made a couple of suggestions, but then so had Elizabeth. And he'd made them in such a way that they weren't threatening.

"What will it be for lunch?" Charlotte rummaged through her refrigerator's meat drawer. "We have bologna or . . ." she almost groaned, "bologna."

"I'm really up for some bologna. What about you, Elizabeth?"

Charlotte watched her daughter giggle. "Mom knows I like it. Oh no! We're out of sodas."

"So you'll drink milk." Charlotte took six slices of bread from a cellophane wrapper.

"But what about Mr. McQuade?"

"Hey, I drink milk all the time. But I'll tell you what. If it's all right with your mother, we can get some sodas for later. I'll spring for them if you make the trip to the store."

"Sure," Elizabeth agreed readily, before she turned to Charlotte, almost as an afterthought. "That okay with you, Mom?"

"Sure," she parroted her daughter. Hadn't the little "mom and pop" store two blocks away been one of the pluses about their house that she'd pointed out to Elizabeth? Elizabeth and Mac disappeared into the living room for him to get money out of his sweat jacket. Mac returned alone and leaned lazily against the counter. Charlotte assumed Elizabeth was on her way to Cleary's.

"You didn't have to do that."

"What, pay for the drinks or send Elizabeth away?"

Charlotte looked up, a knife smeared with mustard in her hand. She hadn't even thought about them being alone before he'd mentioned it. But now she did, and the memory of what had happened earlier came rushing into her mind, pinkening her cheeks.

"The drinks. I could have paid for them." Charlotte was pleased that her voice remained steady.

"It was the least I could do since you're providing such a great lunch." Mac snatched up the piece of cheese she'd just sliced and stuck it in his mouth. "Mmmm, good."

Charlotte glared at him as she carried the three plates to the table. She doubted he saw her since he was pulling the milk out of the refrigerator, but it made her feel better.

"May I ask you a question?" Mac poured milk for all of them and plunged ahead, not waiting for her answer. Maybe he thought she'd say no. "Why are you so against taking any help from me?"

Charlotte stopped folding the napkins and looked up. "I take help from you."

Mac carried the glasses to the table. "You do when it's for Elizabeth. But when it's just me, Mac McQuade trying to do something for Charlotte Handley, you don't want it."

"That's ridiculous." Charlotte found a bag of chips and tore them open with a vengeance. What was it with this man? First he comes into her house and kisses her crazy, then he sets himself up as some amateur psychologist. "You helped me today, didn't you?" she pointed out logically.

"Yeah, but you didn't like it."

"I like to do things for myself." Maybe he wasn't an amateur. He certainly had her pegged.

"An admirable trait."

"But?" The way he had said "an admirable trait" there had to be a "but" attached to it.

Mac smiled and took another piece of cheese. "But there's nothing wrong with taking a little help now and then. Everybody needs it."

Charlotte gazed into his clear, blue-green eyes and caught a glimmer of the same vulnerability she'd noticed when she'd awakened him in his school room. She wondered what kind of help he'd needed—and hoped someone had been there to give it to him.

Mac jumped to his feet. "Come on, let's measure another strip while we wait for Elizabeth." He was getting entirely too involved with this woman. Helping her out was one thing. Hell, taking her out was one thing. But psychoanalyzing her, now that was something else again. She liked to do things for herself. So what? Lots of people were independent. But Mac didn't think she'd always been that way, and he wondered if she was carrying it a little too far.

"Anxious to be finished, huh?" Charlotte took the pencil from behind her ear and marked the wallpaper. "Maybe you're the one who's sorry he got himself roped into helping."

Mac used the razor to cut along the straight edge. "I didn't get roped into it," he answered with feigned indignation. "I volunteered. Besides." He lifted his head, and his sensual gaze drifted slowly over Charlotte. "I can only think of one or two things I'd rather be doing than helping to spread these cheery flowers over your kitchen."

Oh yeah, thought Charlotte, and I'll bet I know what one of them is. In an attempt to keep at bay the memory of his hard, hot body pressed against her softness, she searched for another topic.

"Why *did* you stop by today? Elizabeth didn't tell you we were wallpapering, did she?" Charlotte was going to have a serious talk with her daughter if she had.

Mac chuckled. "No. I stopped by to ask you a question." He watched her blue eyes narrow.

"What question?"

He leaned back against the counter. "Have you heard about the school's autumn dance?"

Had she? That was practically all Elizabeth talked about since Todd Parks, her algebra tutor, asked her to go with him. But why would Mac McQuade want to know that? "I believe Elizabeth has mentioned it."

"Is she going?"

"Yes."

"Good." Not only was he glad for Elizabeth's sake, but it made what he was about to do easier. "I'm going, too—as a chaperone. It's part of my job."

"I see." Charlotte wasn't at all sure where this was leading.

"How about going with me?"

"Me?" Was Mac McQuade asking her to a high school dance?

"Of course you." Didn't the woman know when she was being asked out?

"Oh, I don't think—"

"We need more chaperones." Why was he telling her that? There were plenty of parents and teachers to watch the kids. Because, dammit, she had been going to turn him down.

"Need more chaperones for what?" Elizabeth banged open the backdoor, allowing a few crinkly leaves to skitter across the kitchen floor.

"Mr. McQuade and I were just discussing the autumn dance."

"Aren't there enough chaperones?" Elizabeth seemed truly concerned.

Mac felt a pang of guilt. All he'd meant to do was make it easier for Charlotte to accept the idea of going out with him. "Actually, I just asked your mother to go with me."

"Oh." Charlotte could feel Elizabeth's eyes watching her. "Are you going?"

"Well, I don't know . . ."

"Aw, come on, Mom. It'll be fun."

"And you'll be doing the school a service." Mac was surprised he didn't choke over this exaggeration. What was wrong with him, anyway? He didn't usually have to coerce women into going out with him. But then he usually didn't care that much one way or the other. Not like this anyway. He found himself worrying about just what he was going to try next if she refused him.

How had she gotten into this spot? Charlotte thought. All she'd wanted to do was finish her degree and make a good home for herself and Elizabeth. Men were definitely not in her plans. But ever since she'd seen Mac McQuade standing in the front of his classroom, a scaly fish hanging around his neck, she hadn't been able to get him out of her mind.

Charlotte sensed everyone waiting for her answer. Oh well, it was only a school dance—and they were going as chaperones. What could happen? She forced thoughts of his kiss from her mind.

"I'd love to go."

"Good." Mac let out a breath he hadn't realized he was holding. "What do you say we eat those bologna sandwiches so we can hurry up and finish this room? Unless, of course, you two like it this way."

Looking around the room, Charlotte laughed. While the walls that had been papered were neat enough— not professional neat, but certainly amateur neat—the rest of the room would qualify as a disaster area. Wads of leftover paper lay like mummified soccer balls where they'd fallen; scissors, seam rollers, plumbs, and yardsticks, all the tools of the wallpapering trade, littered the floor.

Charlotte cocked her head to one side, whisking away a curly tendril of hair that had escaped her kerchief. "Well, I think I could live with it, but I don't know about my mother."

Mac washed down a bite of sandwich with his milk. "Your mother is going to live here?" Somehow, after hearing Elizabeth talk about Charlotte, he hadn't thought her the type to go running home to her mother, or in this case bring her mother to her. What happened to all that hard won independence?

"Grandma is coming for Thanksgiving," Elizabeth piped in. "Mom asked her last week and she called Friday night to say she would. That's why Mom is so hot to get this room finished."

"Oh, it is not." Charlotte stopped scraping the last of her sandwich into the garbage. "I told you last week we were going to wallpaper today—and that was before I even spoke with your grandmother."

"Yeah, well, you said it, but I guess I didn't believe you." Elizabeth bent over and pulled a strip of wallpaper from the bottom of her shoe.

Charlotte just rolled her eyes heavenward. Teenagers. But as much as she hated to admit it, Elizabeth had a point. Charlotte did want the house, Elizabeth, everything, looking its best when her mother arrived from Everettsville. Maybe then she'd believe that Charlotte was capable of handling her life without Brian. Without Brian's money or influence.

"Hand me the razor, will you, Charlotte?"

She looked around to see Mac on the step chair smoothing out the section of paper they'd measured while Elizabeth was gone. He hadn't been kidding about being in a hurry to finish. Of course, who could blame him? Wallpapering was hardly the type of chore you helped a virtual stranger with, especially without some kind of compensation.

Well, she didn't have the money to pay him and—her eyes flew open. He wouldn't expect—would he? Not at a high school dance. But what about after the dance, a pesky little voice questioned. Don't be silly. He'll bring me home, straight home. And Elizabeth will be here.

Besides, Brian had always told her how frigid she was. Nobody wanted a cold woman. Ah, but you melted pretty quickly when Mac kissed you, that stupid voice reminded. A fluke. It would never happen again. I'll see that it never gets a chance to happen again.

"I think it's under that roll beside the sink."

"What?" Charlotte blinked back to the present.

Mac twisted his head around. "The razor, look under that wallpaper." He motioned with his elbow.

"Oh, sure." *Get a hold of yourself, Charlotte.* He's going to think your daughter has a moron for a mother. Charlotte handed him the tool, acknowledging his thanks and stood back to watch him trim away the excess paper. What a silly goose she was being. No one with a tush like that would be interested in anything that quiet, little Charlotte Handley had to offer.

By five o'clock the room was finished and most of the scraps had been cleaned up. Charlotte followed Mac into the living room. Elizabeth had already disappeared into the bathroom for what Charlotte was certain would be a hot-water-depleting shower.

"I can't thank you enough for your help." Charlotte leaned against the doorjamb, watching Mac pull on a sweatshirt jacket with a barely discernible college emblem embossed on the front. "I'm not certain Elizabeth and I could have done it by ourselves."

"Sure you could." Mac zipped up the jacket. "I hardly offered more than moral support."

Charlotte shook her head, realizing she still had her hair wrapped in that awful scarf. She yanked it off. "Well, regardless of what you say, we are grateful." His words, however unfair they were to him, had warmed her heart.

"It was my pleasure." Their gazes met and locked.

"Listen," Charlotte heard herself say. "I can't offer you much, but I hate to send a man who has worked so hard away hungry. Why don't you stay for dinner. I could run to the store and get some—"

"I can't."

"Oh . . . well, sure. I understand. It was just an idea." Charlotte caught herself wringing her hands and stuffed them into her jeans pockets. What had ever possessed her to ask him to dinner? To her recollection, she'd never done anything like that before—not even with Brian. Some policies were better left unchanged.

"I'd like to, Charlotte, really. It's just that I have a previous commitment." Mac felt like kicking himself. She had no idea how he hated to leave, but he had no choice. Her invitation had surprised him. If her reaction was any indication, it had surprised her, too. And oh, how he wanted to take her up on it.

"Of course. I understand." Was she repeating herself? What a ninny she was. Only she would think that a man like this didn't have a date on Saturday night. Charlotte just wished he'd leave, so she could go lick her wounds in private. But he wasn't leaving.

Charlotte watched as he moved around the tweed armchair, stalking her like a jungle cat. He stopped just short of touching her. "I really would like to stay, Charlotte." The breath from his words wafted cross her cheek as his finger lifted her chin. The same finger caressed her lips when she tried to speak. "And please don't tell me you understand."

Charlotte swallowed, trying to ignore the welcome warmth that radiated from him, trying to ignore her body's desire to arch toward that sizzling heat. "But I do." Her voice was a husky whisper.

Mac grinned. "We'll talk about it Friday."

"Friday? . . . Oh, we're chaperoning the dance." When he smiled, the laugh lines fanning his eyes deepened, the dimples appeared.

He nodded, slowly. "There's just one problem, Charlotte." Mac lost the battle he'd been fighting with himself and moved closer to her.

"What?" Her breasts, now pebble hard, pressed into his chest.

"Who's going to chaperone the chaperones?" His lips, which had barely brushed her when he spoke, now punctuated his question with a deep, soul-searching kiss.

Charlotte tried to remember she was frigid, but her bones had turned to warm molasses and so had her brain it appeared. She could do nothing but feel. Mac's tongue plumbed the depths of her mouth; his large sensitive hands, rough from wallpapering, sent shivers down her back. His body, hard and pulsing with desire, cradled her own.

Mac lifted his head, trying hard to steady his breathing. What was he doing? This woman's teen-aged daughter could emerge from the bathroom any second. He was covered with paste and dirt, as was Charlotte, and he had an appointment in an hour that he felt morally obligated to keep. And all he could think of was how much he wanted to strip Charlotte naked and slide into her moist heat.

He backed up, ramming his hands in the sweatshirt pockets to keep from touching her again. "I'll pick you up at seven-thirty," he said, never breaking stride as he escaped through the door.

"Okay. Thanks again." Charlotte's words echoed in the now empty room. Her fingers skimmed her lips. They felt thoroughly kissed. What had she gotten herself in to? And more important, how was she ever going to get herself out?

Mac kicked his front door shut and reached for the light switch. A warm glow bathed the spacious room that served as a combination living room/office. Book-lined walls surrounded the huge fieldstone fireplace, forming a solid contrast to the floor to ceiling windows that offered a panorama of the York River.

Ever since he'd bought this house, he'd found its quiet beauty and strength comforting. The property had been way too rich for his salary, but then Mac didn't really need the money he made from teaching. "A good thing," he mumbled to himself as he reached inside the refrigerator for a beer.

"To being born with a silver spoon in your mouth." He raised the bottle in mock salute as he settled down on the sofa. But five minutes later he was up again, pacing. He usually felt so at peace when he returned from the V. A. hospital. His weekly visits with the men had become a ritual. And though Mac was there to cheer them up, he always felt he got as much as he gave. But not tonight.

"Damn!" All he could think about tonight was blue eyes, red hair, and a sweetness he'd never known before. Mac flopped back onto the overstuffed couch wishing Charlotte were there with him to make his house less lonely. They could sit together, their legs entwined, and wait for the first rays of dawn to dust the river with diamonds. He almost ached to share that with her. Mac had never felt this longing, that went beyond the physical before, and it worried him more than a little.

Well, whatever caused this feeling, he wanted to be with her. Friday night couldn't arrive fast enough for him.

_____ FIVE _____

Friday night had come too quickly.

Charlotte stood in front of the bathroom mirror trying her best to apply sable brown mascara to her long, thick lashes and wondering how she had let it come to this. All week she'd been tempted to call Mac McQuade with some excuse why she couldn't chaperone the dance with him.

The president needs me to help negotiate world peace; our house has been hit by a fluke outbreak of the plague; slimy, outerspace creatures have eaten all my clothes. Her mind had worked tirelessly on the problem, allowing little time for anything else.

Quality studying time had been almost nonexistent, although somehow she'd managed to make a B and elicit a positive comment from her English professor. Maybe she worked better when her brain was preoccupied. She hoped not. After tonight, she positively refused to give Mac another thought.

This was it. The last time she'd see him. The last time she'd think of him. She was going to the dance tonight simply because she couldn't come up with a logical reason not to, but no more. Her life didn't need a man complicating the works. Especially one that made her feel the way Mac did.

"Mom, have you seen my black handbag?" Elizabeth's excited voice vibrated through the bathroom door.

"*My* black handbag is on your bed, where I told you I'd put it."

"Gee, thanks, Mom." Elizabeth burst through the door.

So much for privacy. Charlotte started to give her fifty cents lecture on knocking, but decided as cloud-bound as Elizabeth was, she'd never remember it. Besides, Elizabeth had already flown from the room. And Charlotte had spent enough time primping. What was she getting all dolled up for anyway?

Charlotte gave herself one last critical survey in the mirror. Hair, too colorful and curly, almost wild. Nothing she could do about that. Eyes, undoubtedly her best feature, and the mascara had helped to accentuate them. Nose, what could you say about a nose? Mouth. Oops. Charlotte searched through her makeup case for the lipstick she'd forgotten to apply. There, that looked better, though she thought her lips nothing extraordinary.

Until Mac kisses them.

That was it. One of those little gems that kept springing into her mind at the most unexpected times. Charlotte jammed the lipstick into her makeup case. It was all because of what Mac had said about who was going to chaperone the chaperones. Those words enveloped her like the poignant smell of burning wood that escaped Williamsburg's chimneys. But were they a threat . . . or a promise?

"You look great, Mom." Charlotte had walked into Elizabeth's poster-lined room.

"Me! What about you?"

Elizabeth twirled around, wobbling slightly on the unaccustomed heels. "It is pretty, isn't it?" She smoothed out the skirt of her royal blue dress and smiled up at her mother.

"The dress is lovely." Charlotte brushed one of Elizabeth's curls behind her ear. "But then so are you."

"Aw, Mom." Color rose in Elizabeth's already flushed cheeks. "Do you really think Todd will like it?"

"He'd better." Charlotte gave Elizabeth a guick hug. They had gone to Richmond for the dress, and it had cost a lot more than Charlotte had wanted to pay. But when she'd seen Elizabeth's eyes light up . . . well, peanut butter sandwiches were just as nutritious as meat.

"I think Mr. McQuade will like your dress, too, Mom."

Charlotte laughed. "That's not what you said before."

"Well, I guess I wanted you to buy a new one."

"This one is fine." Charlotte had on her light blue wool dress. The lines were simple, and she had always thought it flattered her slender figure.

"Yeah, you're right. And the scarf looks good, too."

"Do I have this thing tied right?"

The mellow chimes of the doorbell interrupted Elizabeth's answer.

"Which one do you think it is?" Elizabeth's eyes were as big as saucers.

"Maybe we should answer the door and find out," Charlotte teased. She linked her arm through Elizabeth's and walked toward the living room. But even though she hoped she appeared a lot calmer than her daughter, Charlotte seriously doubted Elizabeth's heart beat any faster than her own.

Charlotte hung back in the hallway, letting Elizabeth open the door so Todd wouldn't be overwhelmed by redheaded women. She heard her daughter say, "Oh, it's you, Mr. McQuade. Hi."

Mac stepped into the living room. "That greeting didn't do much for my ego, especially coming from such a gorgeous young lady." Mac grinned and Elizabeth turned scarlet.

"Aw, Mr. McQuade, I thought you might be Todd."

"I figured as much." Mac glanced around the room. "Is your mother ready?"

"I'm right here." Charlotte stood in the shadows trying to muster the courage to walk into the living room. He looked so handsome. His navy blue blazer and blue oxford shirt did wonderful things for his eyes and tanned skin. She quickly checked his tie, only a tad disappointed that it sported a paisley print rather than scales. Smiling at her silly thought, she stepped into the room.

"Hi." His single word slid over her as provocatively as his gaze.

"Hi." Charlotte wondered if even Elizabeth and Todd's conversation would be this inane.

"You look beautiful." Mac smiled. Friday had been worth the wait.

"Thank you." Charlotte glanced down. "Are those for me?"

"Oh . . . yes." Mac held out the half dozen white roses he clutched. What in the hell was the matter with him? He was acting like a teenager on his first date. She just looked so glorious with her hair rivaling the fiery maple leaves and her skin dewy and flawless as the rose petals. Boy, had he missed seeing her.

"He's here." Charlotte and Mac glanced over to where Elizabeth stood, plastered to the window.

"Maybe we better go put these in some water." Charlotte motioned toward the kitchen.

"Looks good." Mac surveyed the newly wallpapered walls till his eyes snagged on Charlotte's bottom as she bent over to get a vase from underneath the sink.

Charlotte stood up and turned and Mac's stare snapped back to the calico flowers. "It does, doesn't it?" Charlotte turned on the tap. "Thanks in large part to you."

Mac started to deny that he'd been much help at all, but Elizabeth came into the kitchen to get Todd's boutonniere out of the refrigerator. Charlotte's attention switched from Mac to her daughter's corsage, a spray of miniature carnations pinned to the shoulder of her dress. After that things seemed pretty hectic as he and Todd helped their dates with their coats. Yep, no doubt about it, Mac felt just like a teenager.

"Now remember, Elizabeth." Charlotte caught her daughter before the door closed behind her.

"I know, Mom. Be home by eleven-thirty. Honestly, you'd think I was Cinderella or something."

"Elizabeth."

"Okay, okay. I was just teasing." Elizabeth grabbed her mother's hand, giving it a squeeze. "Have a good time."

"You too, Lizzy."

Charlotte watched them walk down the pavement toward Todd's borrowed Hyundai.

"You're not worried are you?" Mac draped his arm around Charlotte's shoulders.

She looked up into his handsome face, luxuriating in the solid, comforting feel of him. "Maybe just a little. This is her first date in a car."

"She'll be fine."

Charlotte nodded.

"Todd's a nice boy."

"I know."

"And." Mac leaned over and brushed his lips across her forehead. "It's not as if we won't be right there to watch her."

Charlotte tried to suppress a giggle, then let go with a full, musical laugh that warmed Mac's soul. "You know, you're right. What do you say we get to chaperoning?"

"This is the gym?" Charlotte gazed around in awe as they entered the school dance.

"Looks different, doesn't it?" Mac took her coat and folded it over a bleacher. "The students really go all out with the decorations."

"I'll say they do." Silver paper shimmered on the walls, while a rainbow of balloons canopied the dancers. And everywhere blue and white crepe paper streamers fluttered and swayed in time to the music.

Charlotte followed Mac as he led the way toward a group of people standing against the wall across from the band. Judging from their ages and their obvious dislike of the loud, pulsating music, she supposed they were her fellow chaperones. They greeted Mac, and he moved down the row introducing Charlotte.

Miss Zeller didn't seem to recognize her as Elizabeth's mother, a fact that pleased Charlotte. The last thing she wanted now was a parent-teacher conference to discuss algebra.

Mac leaned against a poorly disguised balance beam and pulled Charlotte closer to him, almost yelling in her ear to be heard above the music. "Now aren't you having fun?"

"Sure beats aliens eating my clothes. No, never mind." She waved off his questioning expression. "Yes, I'm having a great time."

Now that she was officially part of the line-up—was there some unwritten law that said the chaperones had to stand like this?—Charlotte began searching the room for her daughter.

"She's over there." Mac pointed out Elizabeth and Todd flailing around to the band's rendition of a current George Michael hit.

"She's a pretty good dancer. Maybe all those years of ballet lessons were worth it."

"How about her mother?"

Charlotte looked up at Mac, disturbingly aware that he stood very close and that he still held her hand. "Oh, I never had ballet lessons."

"But do you like to dance?"

Charlotte couldn't remember the last time she had, but she guessed she liked it okay and told him.

"Would you like to?"

Charlotte's eyes jerked from the hypnotizing depths of his to the crowded gym floor. "Here? Now?"

"Sure. There's no law that says the chaperones have to stand here in a line."

He was reading her mind again. "Oh, I don't think I could."

"You're probably right—about both of us. We'll wait for a slow dance." He bobbed his brows suggestively. "I like those better anyway."

"Mac."

Charlotte didn't think she'd ever heard a name spoken so . . . so provocatively and peeked around Mac to see who owned the come hither voice. She should have known. The sleek, sexy blonde she'd noticed talking to Mac at the parade stood on the other side of him.

Up close she appeared even sleeker and sexier. It might have been her silhouette-hugging black knit dress, or maybe it was the sleek curves it hugged. Whatever the reason, Charlotte suddenly felt—what was Elizabeth's word?—frumpy.

"How are you doing, Cynthia?"

Charlotte shot Mac a quick glance and cringed when she saw the roguish grin plastered to his face. Sleek, sexy Cynthia noticed it, too, because she gave him a sex starlet smile before her eyes slid to Charlotte.

"I'm fine, Mac. And you?"

Mac slung his arm around Charlotte's shoulder. The act both surprised and, oddly enough, pleased her.

"Great. Cynthia, I don't believe you've met Charlotte Handley. Charlotte, this is Cynthia Fields. She teaches here." Mac's fingers gently squeezed Charlotte's warm, wool-covered arm.

"Elizabeth Handley is your daughter, isn't she?"

"Why, yes," Charlotte answered, trying to ignore the critical appraisal the other woman gave her. "How did you know?"

"Oh, Pat Zeller told me our Mac was dating one of the students' mothers."

Charlotte felt heated blood rush to her cheeks. She strongly suspected that Sexy Cynthia had told her that choice morsel of gossip to be catty, yet the fact remained that she didn't want people thinking she and her daughter's teacher were an item. Especially when it wasn't true. Her peripheral vision caught a glimpse of Mac's strong, lean fingers tightening around her arm and her spirits plummeted. She'd be hard pressed to find anyone here tonight that didn't believe the rumor. Heck, she had a hard time not accepting it herself.

"You'll have to excuse us, Cynthia. I promised Charlotte I'd dance the slow songs with her."

Charlotte didn't have time to deny Mac's statement before he pulled her onto the gym floor. Once they were there, she had little choice but to step into his arms and follow his lead.

"Why did you do that?" Charlotte tilted her head so she could look up at him.

"I didn't get the impression you had any great desire to continue our conversation with Cynthia. Was I wrong?" Mac guided her adroitly past a couple stuck together like gum on a shoe. Charlotte made sure they weren't Elizabeth and Todd.

"I really didn't care one way or the other. You seemed to be enjoying her . . . conversation." Now who was being catty?

Mac pulled away just enough to look down into her face. Charlotte felt his eyes on her, and against her will, she met his gaze. His didn't waver. "Cynthia and I dated a few times when she first transferred here."

"You don't owe me an explanation. I—"

"I know I don't *owe* you one." The corners of his mouth turned up, but his eyes remained serious. "Anyway, we went out a couple of times. Then I stopped calling, she started dating some judo instructor, and that was that. It was never anything serious— for either of us."

Maybe he didn't think so, but Charlotte had noticed the way Sexy Cynthia had almost licked her chops when she'd looked at Mac. The signals the woman had been sending were clear to Charlotte, and she didn't even own a code book. Oh, well, Mac McQuade's love life, or lack there of, was certainly no concern of hers. The only thing they were doing was chaperoning a school dance.

Funny, how she kept having to remind herself of that. Moving around the floor in his arms to the sultry sounds of the keyboard and bass made her almost forget. He didn't hold her a fraction of an inch closer than propriety dictated, yet she tingled everyplace their bodies touched. His arm circling her ribs, the gentle guiding pressure of his hand at the small of her back, the occasional brushing of his chest against hers, all sent a delicious languid warmth through her.

It took the jarring chords of a Led Zeppelin classic to break the spell and send them scurrying off the dance floor. "Not up to trying your luck with Heavy Metal, huh?" Mac chuckled as they reached the infamous "line up" wall.

"Not in front of all these kids." She'd never noticed how primitive and sexual a drum beat could be.

Mac scanned the sea of agile, gyrating bodies. "They can be pretty intimidating. Someday I'll take you to this little place I know in Richmond. They have live bands." He leaned over toward her ear, tickling the tiny tendrils away with his hot breath. "And they accommodate us older folks—only play golden oldies from the sixties and seventies."

Even though she'd lived in Richmond for over fifteen years, Charlotte was certain she'd never been to the place he described. Most likely it wasn't on Brian's list of acceptable hangouts for an up-and-coming doctor to frequent. But it sounded fascinating.

Charlotte could almost visualize the intimate, dimly-lit hideaway, smell the earthy combination of cigarette smoke and human sweat, hear the soulful refrain of Bill Withers', "Lean on Me" . . . .

"Do you remember this song?"

Charlotte blinked and swallowed quickly. No wonder her imagination had seemed so real. The five member band, their glitzy costumes identifying them immediately as a nineties group, was now playing an up-dated version of "Lean on Me." Boy, was she going to have to watch the line between her fantasies and reality. They had a tendency to blend whenever she encountered Mac.

She listened for a moment, engulfed in the sights, sounds, and smells of her past. "Sure I do. I even recall the first time I heard it. It was September of seventy-two, I had just arrived on campus." Charlotte glanced up at him. "The University of Virginia," she explained. "Well, anyway, there I was, this little country girl from Everettsville, who'd never been anywhere, but who'd somehow managed to get herself a scholarship. Nobody in my family had ever been to college, and I was *so* scared." Charlotte shook her head at the memory.

"So anyway, I started walking across campus, to try and acclimate myself, and I noticed a group of people gathered close to a dorm. They all seemed to know each other, and to be having a good time. As I went closer, I heard 'Lean on Me'—someone had a window open and the radio was turned up really loud."

"And it made you feel like you belonged, right?" Mac interjected, not liking to think of her alone and afraid.

"No. Actually, I took one look at the other students, wondered what in the heck I thought I was doing there, and headed straight back to my dorm room."

Charlotte laughed, but Mac didn't think it was funny, and he didn't think she thought so either. "How long were you at U.Va.?"

"Not long," Charlotte sighed. "I met Brian right after semester break my freshman year. We were married that June."

"Were your parents disappointed?"

"It was just my mother by that time, and no, I think she was glad. Brian impressed her. He was going to be a doctor, and his family had a lot of money." Her eyes met his. "Mine didn't."

"Were you ever tempted to go back and finish your degree?"

Charlotte shook her head, trying not to sound sorry for herself. "Brian was in medical school, and he wanted me with him. Then I had Elizabeth, and well . . . I just got caught up in other things." Brian's things, she thought, but didn't say it out loud.

"But you're doing it now," he said, and Charlotte could have sworn she heard pride in his voice.

"Yes." Charlotte leaned against the wall. How had hearing one old song precipitated her telling Mac her life story? His was the one she wanted to know. "What were you doing in seventy-two?"

Charlotte could sense him stiffening, even though they weren't touching. "I was in 'Nam."

It was there again—that underlying vulnerability and sadness in the depths of his beautiful blue-green eyes. The Vietnam War hadn't much affected Charlotte personally. Oh, she had read the *Newsweek* articles, and watched the protesters on the nightly news, but through most of the war, Brian had a student deferment. And even without that, his asthma kept him safe from the draft.

But Charlotte had heard about what the young soldiers had to endure from Mildred, her mother-in-law's cleaning lady. And she had grieved with the old black woman when her grandson was sent home in a body bag. Memories of the letters Mildred had read to her came flooding back and she cringed to think that Mac had lived through that or worse.

She touched his sleeve, conscious of the solid strength of his arm under the cloth. "Was it so awful?"

"Yeah, it was bad." Mac looked down into the sweet, gentle face he was beginning to care about very much, and wondered what she would think if she knew of the torture and humiliation he'd been forced to endure. God, he wanted to spare her that.

"Come on," he said grabbing Charlotte's hand, the one that had touched his sleeve so comfortingly. "You haven't met the principal yet. And that's a thrill no one should miss."

She not only met Mr. Porterfield, the principal, she danced with him. He was a short, rotund man with bright blue suspenders that proudly proclaimed his school's name. His two left feet left imprints on Charlotte's shoes. But even his constant flow of good-hearted humor couldn't rid her mind of questions. What had happened to Mac in Vietnam and why wouldn't he tell her about it?

By quarter of eleven the crush of bodies was beginning to thin out. Mac had managed to find them a cup of coffee someplace, and they sat on a rolled up gym mat savoring the chance to get off their feet. Charlotte saw Elizabeth headed their way and became instantly wary. The few other times their paths had crossed this evening, Elizabeth had seemed content to act as though they were nothing more than passing acquaintances.

The first time this had happened, Charlotte and

Mac had been dancing. "Do you think Elizabeth is embarrassed because I'm here?" Charlotte had asked Mac. Being in Mac's arms, moving to the sensual strains of a love ballad, had made Charlotte feel very mellow.

Mac had twisted around to look in the direction she had pointed with their linked hands, and shrugged. Every cell in Charlotte's body had been aware of that motion. "I don't know. She wanted you to come." He'd searched her face. "Does it bother you?"

"Hmm. I guess not." She'd put her cheek back on his shoulder and let him lead her around the gym.

Now, relaxing on the mat, sipping her coffee, Charlotte tilted her head back and stared at Elizabeth.

"Hi, Mom! Are you having a good time?"

Charlotte resisted the urge to ask Elizabeth what she wanted. She hadn't been a mother for fourteen years without recognizing the signs. "Sure. How about you?"

"Oh, I'm having a great time." Elizabeth's smile shifted to Mac. "How about you, Mr. McQuade?"

"Terrific!" Mac smiled back and Charlotte wondered if he realized he'd become part of the setup.

"Good." Elizabeth sank down on the red plastic. "Listen, Mom, I know we talked about my being home around eleven-thirty."

"Exactly eleven-thirty."

"Huh?" Elizabeth gave her a puzzled look.

"There was no around about it. We agreed on eleven-thirty."

"Well, yeah, but listen." Elizabeth stopped for breath. "Now, don't say no till you've heard me out. There's this really neat girl named Melissa Applegate."

She twisted around her mother. "You know Melissa, don't you, Mr. McQuade?" Apparently it was a rhetorical question because she rushed on without giving him a chance to answer. "Well, anyway she's having this really neat party after the dance. And do you know what?"

Charlotte managed a quick "what," on her guard after Mac's inability to answer his question.

"She asked Todd and me to come. Now I know it's short notice, and Melissa explained that. Her mother just told her today that she could invite more kids and she didn't have my phone number, and, oh Mom, can I please go? Please?"

"Oh, Lizzy, I don't know."

"Don't say no, Mom, please! All I'm asking for is a half hour, just thirty more little minutes."

"Where does she live?" Charlotte asked feeling Elizabeth's death grip on her hand slacken. Was it that obvious that she was sending up the white flag so quickly?

"It's real close to the school."

"Yes, but where exactly?"

Elizabeth's face fell. "I don't know *exactly*. But Todd does. He's been there before and he says it's not far."

"Are her parents going to be there?"

"Oh, yes. And they're nice people, very responsible."

Charlotte doubted Elizabeth would know them if they drifted down through the balloons this very moment, but there would be nothing to be gained by pushing the issue. She was either going to let her go or not. It was too late for references. Unless . . . .

Charlotte stole a quick peek at Mac, but he suddenly seemed to be taking his chaperoning duties very seriously and was scrutinizing the few remaining dancers. Well, it wasn't his decision to make anyway. It was hers.

"Oh, all right." Charlotte caught her daughter's hand before she could jump up. "But be home by midnight little Cinderlizzy, or you'll have more than a pumpkin and a few mice to worry about."

"Thanks, Mom. You won't be sorry. Well, I better go."

She was already sorry. Darn, she'd hated it when Brian had made all the decisions for her, but making them all herself was no fun either. It would be nice to have someone with whom to share the process. What she needed was a person to sit down with and talk over alternatives before jointly deciding the best plan of action.

Again her gaze slid toward Mac, but this time he stared back at her, and she quickly looked away. What was she thinking? Mac McQuade and she had chaperoned a high school dance together. That was hardly tantamount to creating a co-parenting group.

Charlotte watched Elizabeth as she told Todd the good news. They both left through the gym doors to find their coats before driving off to the party of Neat Melissa with the nice, responsible parents.

Charlotte squirmed around on the rolled-up mat to face Mac. "Well, do you?"

Mac had been watching the play of emotions on Charlotte's pretty face run the gamut from uncertain to worried. The determination he saw and heard in her voice now startled him. "Do I what?"

"Know this girl, Melissa Applegate?"

"Not really," he shrugged.

"Why didn't you say so?" she demanded, her voice rising.

Mac's eyes narrowed. "Because, Charlotte, I couldn't get a word in edgewise." His expression softened. "Besides, I didn't think you wanted my interference."

Charlotte sighed. "You're right. I'm sorry I yelled. It's just that I'm still not used to this single parent stuff."

Standing in one smooth movement, Mac offered Charlotte his hand. "You're doing fine. There was no right or wrong way to handle that situation. Trust yourself, Charlotte. Your instincts seem pretty good to me."

The band announced their final song and Mac pulled Charlotte into his arms. "I always dance the last dance," he explained when he noticed her surprise. "It's tradition."

"Oh." Charlotte slipped her arm over his shoulder, resting her hand just below where his collar met the strong, tanned column of his neck. Who was she to mess with tradition? Besides, she had developed a definite fondness for dancing with Mac. Maybe it was just being held by him that she found so appealing.

Whichever it was, she'd better enjoy it while she could. After this dance, there would be no more holding. Her life would return to normal. Her goals would be the same as they were before she saw Mac McQuade's fish tie. Once before she'd allowed a man to take over her life. She wasn't going to make that mistake again. *Mac isn't Brian*, a little voice tried to tell her, but Charlotte listened to the lyrics of the song instead.

Charlotte hadn't realized how stuffy the gym had become until she walked out into the the clear autumn night. The scent of burning wood and dying leaves wafted about them, and Charlotte tucked her hand more securely through Mac's arm. He looked down at her and smiled, their frosted breaths merging between them.

"I don't suppose we have time to go out for a drink or something?"

Charlotte squinted at her watch in the light of an overhead street lamp. Forty-three minutes till the bewitching hour. Hardly enough time to get seated and order a drink. "I'm afraid not." She felt as disappointed as she sounded. "I really should be home when Elizabeth gets there." He seemed to accept her explanation in stride. As she settled into the Jeep's bucket seat Charlotte wondered if he hadn't invited her out of politeness rather than any strong desire to be with her.

By the time they reached her house Charlotte had called herself all kinds of a fool. She wanted their relationship based solely on friendship, right? So what did she care if he felt the same way? That was certainly best.

"What's wrong?"

They were walking toward her front door and Mac's hand had a gentle grip on her elbow.

"Nothing."

"You hardly said two words in the car."

He noticed almost as much as Elizabeth did. They

had reached the small front stoop. "I guess I was just chilly."

Mac wrapped his arms around her waist, snuggling his nose inside the collar of her coat. "You don't feel cold now."

Charlotte tried to remember her "just friends theory." "Maybe I was tired."

Mac's lips traveled up the taut chord of her neck before he erotically nipped her ear lobe. "Too tired to invite me in?"

SIX

Trust your instincts, he'd said. It sounded simple enough. But what did you do when your instincts were at war with each other?

Part of Charlotte, a very powerful part, wanted nothing more than to invite him in—to her house, her life, herself. But another part, call it the self-preservation segment, preached prudence.

Charlotte looked up at Mac. He'd backed away, the only contact between them now were his hands resting lightly on her shoulders. It was almost as if he didn't want his body to influence her decision. But his eyes did. In the pale wash of the porch light, they glowed with a need as strong as her own.

Why not let this evening last a little longer? Elizabeth would be home soon, she reasoned cautiously. And in the meantime, she could enjoy Mac's company.

"Come on." Charlotte fumbled through her handbag for the keys. "I think I owe you something to drink."

Charlotte led the way into the house, pausing only long enough to drop her coat on the sofa before going to the kitchen. Mac followed, loosening his tie as he went.

"I'm afraid I don't have much to offer you." For just a moment, Charlotte thought longingly of the well-stocked bar she'd left behind in Richmond. But she had rarely used it herself, and on her budget, alcohol wasn't a top priority. "Let's see. There's soda." Charlotte moved the jug of milk in her refrigerator, so she could see better. "Or orange juice. *Or* I could make some hot chocolate." She glanced around at Mac.

"That sounds good." His eyes never left her as she moved around the cheery, calico kitchen, bending over to get a saucepan, reaching in the cupboard for the cocoa. He'd never realized cooking could be so damn erotic. She placed the white roses that had reminded him of her skin on the table and smiled at him. Mac almost had to sit on his hands to keep from grabbing her.

"Is it okay?" Charlotte stared across the table at the mug of fragrant, steaming chocolate that he'd barely touched.

"Oh, sure. It's great. Just a little hot." That was an understatement. He'd nearly burned his tongue off when she'd first given it to him. That's what he got for trying to drown his desires in chocolate.

Charlotte found herself wringing her hands and quickly wrapped them around her mug. This was awful. What had made her think she'd enjoy his company? All evening they'd talked and laughed and, she at least, had really had a good time. But now she couldn't think of a thing to say, and when he looked at her like he was now . . . Charlotte jumped up, and bumped the table, causing water to spill out of the vase.

"Would you like some pie? It's pumpkin."

"No."

"Oh." Charlotte put the pie plate down and leaned against the counter, her back to Mac.

"Charlotte."

"What?" The word left her on a breath of air.

"Come here."

Charlotte's eye lids fluttered shut for an instant before she pushed herself away from the cupboard and turned toward Mac. He still sat, but he faced her, his long legs spread in a V. The magnetic pull of eyes now dark with desire, drew her to him.

Charlotte moved toward him, pausing only when her skirt brushed against his pant's leg. Without a word, Mac clasped her slender hips, planting her firmly between his thighs. He buried his face in the soft valley of her breasts.

A soft moan escaped her at the pleasure of his intimate touch. Charlotte wrapped her arms around his neck, weaving her fingers through the thick, brown curls at his nape. Oh, how she'd longed to do that when they'd danced. She dropped her head until it rested on his. His hair was still cold from the night air. The fragrance of fall and his shampoo mingled with the intoxicating scent that was uniquely his, filling her senses.

"Charlotte." His breath warmed her, and the delicious vibrations from his voice ricocheted through her body, softening her bones until she could do nothing but sag against his hardness.

"Oh, God, Charlotte," he whispered against her neck as she slid down to his lap. Colors bright and intense exploded in his brain as he pressed his mouth to hers. Fiery reds, periwinkle blues, and soft, soothing whites. His arms tightened, anchoring her against him as her lips opened and his tongue thrust inside.

Deeper and deeper the whirlwind of sensations took her. She ached for him in ways that startled her in their newness. Her hands needed the feel of him and she outlined the solid curve of his jaw, reveling in the rough abrasion of whiskers. The sound of his moan filled her with joy, and her touch became bolder, following the pulse in his neck until the confining collar of cotton stopped her.

Her innocent touch was driving him mad. Mac tore his mouth away, gasping for breath. Her eyes were open, heavy lidded and nearly indigo with desire. He could see his passion reflected in their dark blue depths. Gently he reached out and touched a tangled red curl. It seemed to crackle and spark between his fingers.

"So beautiful . . . your hair . . . you." His hand caressed her silken cheek. Charlotte turned her head, kissing his palm, wetting it with her tongue, knowing only the need to taste him again.

Tremors surged through his body, and he buried his face in the warmth of her neck while his hand, still tingling from her touch, learned the shape of her breast. It was soft, the tip pebbly hard, and it seemed to swell with his fondling.

"Oh." Her word was little more than a sigh, but it sounded like a siren's call to him. She arched toward him, rubbing her bottom against his hardness.

"Touch me, Charlotte, please."

She dragged her hand slowly, lovingly down his shirt front toward the large, clearly delineated bulge. Her first touch was tentative, but then his mouth crushed down on hers, and his hand thrust under her skirt and she became bolder.

Oh, what was he doing to her? Her heart pounded wildly inside her chest, her shallow breathing came quickly. All the moisture in her body seemed to have pooled between her legs where his finger gently rubbed.

It was so wonderful, the sensations he evoked, the chiming in her head—It was a sixth sense, a mother's sense—the kind that wakes you the moment your child calls out in his sleep—that allowed Charlotte to notice the mantel clock in the living room, marking the midnight hour.

She jerked away, causing Mac to clamp hold of her bottom to keep her from falling.

"What's wrong?" He'd obviously been tangled in the sensual web as thoroughly as she.

"The clock." Charlotte tried to swallow but her mouth was too dry. "It's twelve o'clock." When he still didn't seem to grasp the importance of her announcement, she grabbed his shoulders. "Elizabeth!"

"Oh." Mac made a quick check to assure himself the girl hadn't stolen into the room.

"What are we going to do?" Charlotte tried to

jump up again, but he held her firm. "I must look awful."

Actually, Mac thought she looked great, and sexy as hell, but he didn't imagine debauched was the image she wanted to convey to her daughter. After giving her fanny one last frustrated squeeze, he straightened her panties and pulled down her skirt. "Why don't you go back to your room and straighten up? I'll stay here and answer the door."

"What about you?" Her gaze strayed to the still obvious bulge below his belt.

Mac grinned. "Don't worry about me. I'll use my coat as camouflage if I have to."

Charlotte tried to finger comb her hair, then gave it up as useless. "Okay." She glanced around the room. "Are you sure?"

Mac stood up, brushing a kiss across her forehead. "Go. I'll be fine. And Charlotte?"

"What?"

"Don't forget to rebutton your dress." He didn't even remember opening it. Apparently, he'd been a lot further gone than he'd realized.

Charlotte grabbed the front of her dress, feeling like a vapid Victorian virgin and left the kitchen.

"Oh, my heavens," Charlotte moaned as she glared at the reflection of the wildly aroused woman in her mirror. Was that she? It must be because no one else had hair that red. Charlotte grabbed a brush and tried to tame it. But memories of Mac's fingers twining in her curls while his voice, husky with desire, told her he thought it beautiful, slowed her hand.

"Stop it," she admonished herself. You're a thirty-four year old woman. Certainly old enough to know better than to indulge in heavy petting on a kitchen chair, and now you have to pay the consequences. She threw cold water on her face, hoping it would revive her flushed complexion.

Hurriedly, Charlotte reapplied her makeup and smoothed out her wrinkled skirt, remembering at the last minute to button her dress. That reminded her of what she'd done. Where he'd touched her. Where she'd touched *him*. Charlotte wished with all her might that she didn't have to walk out of the bathroom and face Mac McQuade, but there was no help for it. Hopefully, Elizabeth and Todd would be home soon and then he'd leave.

"Hi."

Charlotte was walking toward the kitchen and hadn't noticed him sitting on her couch until he spoke. She almost skidded to a stop. He looked so at home there—just like he belonged. "Oh, hi."

"I made us some more hot chocolate." He motioned toward the steaming mugs on the coffee table. "Why don't you sit down?"

Beside him? Was he crazy? Charlotte didn't need any more proof that she lost all control when she got near him. On the other hand, she didn't want to look silly, or worse, inexperienced. *He* certainly appeared to be taking their kitchen encounter in stride. You wouldn't know by looking at him now that he had practically begged her to touch his—

"Aren't they home yet?" Charlotte hurried to the window, hoping Mac wouldn't notice the color she was sure flooded her cheeks.

"Nope." He sipped his drink. "But it's only a couple minutes past twelve."

Charlotte peeked around the curtain at the clock. "It's almost quarter after." Two minutes were a couple, or five, maybe, but fifteen—that was late.

"Your chocolate is getting cold."

Charlotte glared at the man comfortably ensconced on her sofa. What was the matter with him? First he acted as if the kitchen affair never happened, then he talked about chilly chocolate when her only child was Lord knew where. Well, it was obvious he wasn't a mother—or a woman either. "You don't have to stay." Did her tone sound as bitchy to him as it did to her?

"Charlotte, honey." The first time she realized he'd moved was when he draped his arm around her shoulders. It wasn't a sensual gesture, just comforting, but it was all she could do not to turn toward him and bury her face in his soft wool jacket. But the new Charlotte wouldn't do that. She couldn't afford to lean on anyone. The only trouble was, Mac didn't seem to realize that. He squeezed her arm and pulled her closer. "She's okay. They probably just had a good time and forgot to watch the clock."

New Charlotte or no, she let herself be held. It felt so wonderful—not like the kitchen affair wonderful—but wonderful all the same. She was almost disappointed when he let her go and asked, "Do you have a deck of cards?"

"Cards? I suppose so." Why did he want to know that?

"Good. Where are they?"

Charlotte indicated the hall table. It wasn't until

she noticed him searching through piles of bills, old receipts, rubber bands, and recipes that she realized she'd let him see her junk drawer. Nobody looked in the junk drawer unless they were a bona fide member of the family. He wasn't. And she just had to stop thinking of him as if he were.

"Found them." He stuffed the papers back into the drawer in an irreverent heap. Just the way they'd been. Charlotte smiled. She thought he might mention the mess. Instead he seemed to accept it, even understand. Were there such things as kindred spirits?

"You do know how to play rummy, don't you?" His question interrupted her thoughts.

"I used to."

"Great." He started rearranging the magazines on the coffee table to give them a playing area. "Oh, it's only fair to warn you that I'm considered somewhat of an expert."

"Really." Charlotte kicked off her pumps and settled across from him on the rug. "Well, maybe I should mention that my mother considered me unbeatable."

Mac cocked a dark brow. "I guess that makes us a good match." With a flair that would put a Las Vegas black jack dealer to shame, he shuffled and dealt the cards.

"Where did you learn to do that?" Charlotte asked, obviously impressed.

"Army," he answered, examining his hand. "Your draw."

Half an hour later they were still playing. He'd only won a few more than half the games, but Charlotte suspected he'd thrown some her way to keep her mind off the time. "It's almost one o'clock."

"Twelve-fifty," Mac corrected, but he didn't seem nearly as nonchalant as he had been earlier.

She ignored his interpretation of the time. "What was that girl's name? The neat one with the responsible parents?"

"Melissa something."

"Applegate. It was Melissa Applegate. Do you think I should call there?"

"Probably wouldn't hurt." Mac moved his outstretched leg from where it had been resting against hers and stood up. He reached down to help her just as the telephone's familiar ring pierced the night silence. Charlotte was on her feet in an instant. It wasn't until she reached the kitchen that she hesitated, but Mac was right beside her and she picked up the receiver before it could sound again.

"Yes. . . . Oh hello, Mrs. Parks. . . ." Mac watched the fear in Charlotte's blue eyes slowly fade. He wished he could do something so it would never have to be there again. "Yes, I know they're late," he heard her say into the phone. "When they left the dance, they were going to a party at Melissa Applegate's house. . . . Oh, it is? . . . Yes, that's probably what happened. . . . I will. . . . Good-bye, Mrs. Parks.

"That was Mrs. Parks."

Mac looked up from the telephone book where he was scanning the As. "So I gathered. What's up?"

"Todd had a twelve o'clock curfew, too." Charlotte sank down on the bar stool. "She did say that Melissa Applegate lives pretty far out Jamestown Road."

"Well, her telephone number's not listed." He shut the phone book.

"What do we do now?" The fear was back in her eyes, but he couldn't help noticing she'd said "we." He wrapped his arms around her.

They both heard the car at the same time. Badly in need of a new muffler, the sound of its engine growled through the sleepy-town quiet. Before they could reach the front door, a contrite looking Elizabeth and a sheepishly apprehensive Todd burst through it.

Ten minutes later, after walking Elizabeth to her room, Charlotte came back into the living room. "Where's Todd?"

Mac dropped the magazine he'd been leafing through. "I just sent him out to warm up the Jeep."

"Thanks for taking him home."

"No problem. He called his mother."

"Good." Charlotte bent over to gather the mugs from the coffee table, but Mac stopped her with a touch of his hand on her shoulder.

"You all right?"

Charlotte nodded. "I'm fine. But next time I'm going to personally check Todd's gas gauge."

"Poor kids. I think they were afraid coming home was going to be worse than being stranded out on Jamestown Road."

"They did look scared," Charlotte laughed. "I was just so glad to see them safe. Besides, I've run out of gas before."

"Me, too," Mac said and grinned.

Charlotte was amazed that as tired as she was, the

sight of his slashing dimples still made her knees weak.

"But when I was in high school," Mac continued, "I ran out of gas on purpose, and ended up in a lot more romantic spot than Jamestown Road."

"You did that a lot, did you?" Charlotte returned his smile. With very little effort Charlotte could imagine him in high school. His frame wouldn't have been quite as broad and muscular; there wouldn't have been the laugh lines or brackets beside his mouth that added character to his handsome face; but the sexy blue-green eyes would have been there, along with the knock-them-dead smile. The girls must have been begging for the chance to run out of gas with him.

"A few times. But I always kept a spare gas can in the trunk."

"Very ingenious." Charlotte could feel him moving toward her.

"Wasn't it though." His body was within a whisper of touching hers. "I'm kind of out of practice, but I'd be glad to show you how I did it."

Out of practice? Charlotte had a feeling that seduction for Mac was like riding a bike—once you knew how, you never forgot. And did he know how. Her heart was already tripping over its next beat, and her mouth was dry. She swallowed. "I think I get the idea. No need to trouble yourself with a demonstration."

"Oh, it would be no trouble." His arms slid around her waist. "But you're right. There are a lot more comfortable places than the back seat of a car."

Just before his lips touched hers, Charlotte's mind began frantically listing them. A bed, the kitchen floor, the couch, a secluded beach, the shower, her coffee table. Her coffee table? Charlotte tried to analyze that last outlandish idea, but her brain shut down.

She felt the bridled passion of his kiss to the tips of her toes. His hands remained at her waist, hers resting lightly on his shoulders. But they both knew what it felt like to touch and be touched. Their lips moved hungrily, their tongues tantalized.

Mac pulled away, his breath coming in ragged gulps. "I better go."

Charlotte nodded, not trusting herself to speak.

"I'll call you."

Charlotte sat in the crowded bus terminal waiting for her mother.

The dispatcher announced the arrival of the one thirty-five from Danville, and Charlotte went out to the loading dock. An unseasonable cold front had whipped down from the north, reminding people that winter wasn't far away, and stripping the trees of all but the staunchest leaves. Charlotte wrapped her scarf more tightly around her neck and dug deeper into her pockets while she waited for her mother to climb off the bus.

Charlotte had wondered if her mother had changed but the moment the slight, graying woman, with a coat to match her hair, descended the steps, she knew she hadn't. It had been nearly fourteen months since they'd seen each other. Charlotte had traveled to Everettsville soon after her divorce. She had hoped for some support—and gotten none.

Charlotte knew now, that it had been ridiculous to think her mother would approve of her actions. No, Ida Smith's reaction to Charlotte's divorce had been nothing but predictable. It wasn't that Ida didn't want her children to be happy; she just didn't think being married to a rich doctor and living in a big house could make anyone unhappy.

"Hi, Mom." Charlotte hugged her mother.

"Charlotte, honey. You look thinner. Are you getting enough to eat?"

"Of course, Mom." Charlotte lead her mother away from the spewing exhaust.

"I need to get my suitcase." Ida looked suspiciously at the bus driver who took luggage from the bus's side compartment.

"I'll get it. Why don't you go ahead to the car? It's around front. I left it open."

"It's colder here than in Everettsville. You should have come home for Thanksgiving, Charlotte." With those words Ida shrugged down into her coat collar and headed for the car.

Charlotte answered a multitude of questions on the short ride home, most of them concerning Elizabeth. When Charlotte realized that in an attempt to convince her mother that Elizabeth was fine, she'd given her daughter epic stature, Charlotte decided to be quiet. Let her wait and see for herself, Charlotte finally decided.

"So this is where you live now." Ida's tone sounded more as if she were viewing cell block C rather than Charlotte's charming little home. Granted, it was nothing like the house in Richmond, but Charlotte wondered if her mother remembered how few times she'd been invited there. Brian had been so opposed to Ida's visits that Charlotte had started taking Elizabeth to Everettsville for holidays. Brian hadn't minded, as long as she scheduled her trips around any parties he wanted her to attend.

"You can stay in here." Charlotte led the way into Elizabeth's room, noting with relief that her daughter had done a commendable job of organizing her accumulation of "things."

"I hate to put anyone out. Where is Elizabeth going to sleep?"

"With me." Charlotte moved the wilting corsage to the bureau so her mother could put her purse on the nightstand.

"You don't have a spare bedroom? Charlotte, honey, in Richmond—"

"No. We only need two." Charlotte forced a smile. "I'll go fix some coffee. Come on out to the kitchen when you're ready." It was going to be a long week.

Two days later Charlotte hadn't changed her mind. At least now that school vacation had started, Elizabeth would be home. Charlotte's mother seemed to be less critical with her granddaughter around. Charlotte just wished Ida could see how truly happy they were.

"These flowers are dead, Charlotte. Where do you want me to throw them?"

Charlotte finished rinsing a glass under the faucet and handed it to Elizabeth to dry. She turned in time to see her mother carrying Mac's roses to the wastebasket. Her roses. Maybe the petals were turning a little brown around the edges, but they were a long way from dead.

Besides, she enjoyed looking at them. Seeing the delicate blooms set off little fantasies in her head. Harmless fantasies, she assured herself. Because nothing would come of them. Mac hadn't called. Just as well, Charlotte thought as she reached out to take the vase moments before her mother dumped the flowers.

"They're still pretty enough. We can use them as a centerpiece for Thanksgiving." Charlotte set the roses back on the table after touching her nose to one. They smelled wonderful and they reminded her of Mac.

"Is that what you bought them for? Thanksgiving?" If her mother was surprised that Charlotte had stopped her from throwing them away, she didn't show it.

"Oh, Mom didn't buy them." Elizabeth hung the towel through the refrigerator door. "Mr. McQuade gave them to her."

Charlotte could feel her mother's eyes examining her and steeled herself for the questions that would start momentarily. Turning back to the sink, Charlotte started wiping the counter. She didn't want to discuss Mac McQuade with her mother, especially since there was nothing to discuss. Obviously Mac was of the same mind as she. After all he hadn't called.

"Who's this Mr. McQuade, Charlotte? You didn't tell me you were dating someone."

Charlotte's denial couldn't be heard above Elizabeth's chatter.

"Mr. McQuade's really great, Grandma. He took Mom to a dance and brought her flowers."

Charlotte scrubbed at a particularly stubborn mustard stain that she knew from experience wasn't going to come out. "We chaperoned a school dance."

"Yeah, and you ought a see him, Grandma." Elizabeth had warmed to her subject and was now sitting across the butcher block table from Ida. "He looks like that guy in the movie about the undercover agent who—"

"I don't get to see many movies."

"Too bad, 'cause he's really a hunk."

A hunk? How did Elizabeth come up with this stuff? Charlotte had to admit it was a fairly accurate description, still . . .

"And he explained the football game to Mom so that I think she actually enjoyed it. Didn't you, Mom?" It must have been another rhetorical question for Charlotte didn't have time to answer before Elizabeth went on. "The other Saturday he came over and helped us wallpaper the kitchen. And he didn't even mind when his clothes got all yukky. Then after the dance he stayed with Mom till I got home. Todd's car—I told you about Todd, didn't I?—well, it ran out of gas and Mr. McQuade drove Todd home."

And he's kind to widows and orphans and takes in stray animals. What was Elizabeth trying to do, nominate him for sainthood? Saint Mac the Hunk. Charlotte smiled in spite of herself.

"Well, he sounds very nice, Charlotte," Ida said, "but don't you think—"

"He is nice," Charlotte broke in halfheartedly,

intending to downplay this whole thing. She could feel her mother's censure; could almost hear her wondering why Charlotte had left a perfectly acceptable marriage, especially since it appeared as though Charlotte wanted a man. During her last visit, Charlotte had insisted that she wanted nothing more to do with the gender.

Yes, she'd make light of the whole thing. Charlotte looked over toward her mother—and her gaze fell on the roses. A warmth spread through her that had nothing to do with the oven being on, or the sexual fantasies that usually accompanied thoughts of Mac.

He *was* nice—and kind and considerate and he'd been wonderful to Elizabeth and her. Heck, he probably did take in strays. *And* he *was* a hunk, possibly the hunkiest man she'd ever met. Elizabeth hadn't said one thing that wasn't true—she hadn't even exaggerated—and Charlotte wasn't going to make Mac out to be something he wasn't just to satisfy her mother.

"Mac McQuade is *very* nice," Charlotte amended, sitting at the table. "He's been a true friend to Elizabeth—and me."

"Yeah, he helped get me a tutor."

Charlotte watched as her mother's eyes moved from Elizabeth back to her. "He's a teacher at Lizzy's high school. As a matter of fact, he teaches her English. Did you know that Elizabeth seems to truly excel in that subject?"

The knock on the back door interrupted Ida's reply. Charlotte glanced at the clock over the stove. The only people who ever came to her back door were Allison and occasionally Sally Reinert. It was too late for Elizabeth's friend, and Sally and her family had already driven to Portsmouth to spend Thanksgiving with her brother.

The rapping sounded again, and Charlotte pushed her chair away from the table. She flicked on the porch light and opened the door. It was more than the frigid night air that made her breath catch.

Charlotte

SEVEN

There in all his hunkish glory stood Mac. He looked cold. The wind had stung his cheeks and nose a ruddy shade, and Charlotte had the strongest desire to step inside his unzipped, brown bomber jacket, snuggle against his rag wool sweater, and warm him up.

"May I come in?" Mac wasn't sure of his reception—after all, he hadn't called—but he didn't expect Charlotte to just stand there staring at him as if he were some figment of her imagination come to life.

"Oh, of course." Charlotte stepped back, allowing him to enter the toasty kitchen. That probably made more sense than wrapping him in her own heat.

"I don't mean to intrude." Mac glanced around the room, returned Elizabeth's friendly smile and noticed the older woman. How could he have forgotten that Charlotte's mother would be here? Turning the Jeep down Charlotte's street seemed even more of an impulsive act than it had before.

"Don't be silly." Charlotte took his jacket. The cold leather contrasted with the lining, warm from his body. His unique, male scent drifted around her, and she forced herself to hang the coat on the peg by the door.

"I hope you don't mind me coming to the back. I noticed the light." Charlotte looked so warm and tempting standing beside him. Her flannel shirt was open at the throat and the sleeves were rolled up. God, he wanted to feel that soft skin against his.

"Don't be silly." Hadn't she just said that? "Come in and sit down."

"Charlotte, honey, aren't you going to introduce me to your friend?"

Charlotte's gaze flew to the table. How could she have forgotten her mother? And worse, how would Mac survive the grilling Ida Smith had in store for him? Charlotte could almost see the questions forming on her mother's lips as she introduced them.

Mac sank onto the kitchen chair wondering why Charlotte's mother looked at him as if he'd burst into the house brandishing smoking six-shooters. The thought struck him again that he shouldn't have come. Maybe he should make his excuses and leave. After all, he did have the long drive up Route 95 to Washington tonight. Mac had almost convinced himself that it wouldn't be the coward's way out when his gaze drifted to Charlotte.

Her perfect porcelain skin appeared pale in the glow of the overhead light, and her blue eyes glowed with concern, but she'd raised her chin to that determined angle he found so appealing. Hell, if she could put up with her mother, so could he.

Mac turned his most socially correct smile toward the older woman. "Charlotte tells me you live in Everettsville."

"Have all my life. Where are you from Mr. McQuade?"

Charlotte's teeth clenched together tightly. She'd known Mac over a month and she'd never delved into his past—well, maybe once she'd asked him about children, but that had just sort of slipped out. Her mother, on the other hand, had known him less than five minutes, and Charlotte knew this first question was merely the tip of the inquisition iceberg.

"New York, Long Island, actually." Mac glanced over at Charlotte, noting her surprise. He guessed he'd never gotten around to telling her where he'd been born. "But I've lived in Williamsburg for about thirteen years."

"Teaching?"

The way Ida said the word Charlotte imagined she didn't consider it in the same league as being a physician. Maybe it wasn't—financially, but there were other considerations. "Mac is an excellent teacher. He's—"

"I'm sure he is, dear. I was just curious. Were your parents teachers, too?"

Mac smiled. Randolph McQuade had endowed schools, not taught in them. "No, ma'am. My father was a businessman and my mother a . . ." He could hardly say society matron, so he settled on the nondescript, "housewife."

Ida's faded blue eyes assessed him with unapologetic

thoroughness. Mac thought she'd have probably made a good Gestapo officer. She leaned back in her chair. "So, I understand you've been seeing my Charlotte."

"Mother!" Charlotte jumped to her feet. This had gone far enough. Quizzing him about his past was one thing. Rude though her mother's questions might be, Mac could always refuse to answer them, or tell her only what he wanted her to know. But insinuating that they were dating—that was too much. What if he thought she'd told her mother that?

"I told you we chaperoned a high school dance." Embarrassed by her mother's questions, not to mention her own outburst, Charlotte turned toward the stove. Grabbing a quilted hot pad she opened the oven door. "Mac, would you like some brownies? Elizabeth made them and they're . . ." Charlotte stared at the gooey brown glob covering the bottom of the pan. "Not done," she finished lamely, slamming the door shut.

"I told you they took thirty-five minutes," Elizabeth piped in.

She'd been so quiet Charlotte had forgotten her daughter was sitting at the table. That and how long it took brownies to bake.

Mac pushed his chair back. "Brownies sound good, but I'm afraid I'll have to take a rain check. I just stopped by to wish you a happy Thanksgiving and to tell you I'd be out of town for a few days." He could tell his presence made Charlotte uncomfortable.

"Oh." Charlotte resisted the urge to ask where he was going. She'd bite off her tongue before she'd succumb to prying like her mother. Or maybe she knew that with Ida Smith around, she wouldn't have to.

"Visiting your parents, Mr. McQuade?"

"No, ma'am." Mac stood and reached for his jacket. "My parents are both dead. I have an uncle who lives outside of Washington. He called, so I thought I'd spend a couple of days with him. He's the only family I have left." Though he answered her mother's question, his gaze never left Charlotte.

Warmth spread through Charlotte when she realized that Mac wanted her to know where he'd be.

"You have a nice trip, Mr. McQuade."

"Thank you, Mrs. Smith. And you have a pleasant stay in Williamsburg." Mac turned to Elizabeth. "See you Monday."

"Sure, Mr. McQuade. Don't eat too much turkey."

"I'll try to watch it," Mac laughed. He shrugged into his coat. "Charlotte, would you walk me to the door?"

Charlotte blinked. What was he talking about? If he took more than one giant step, he'd crash against the door. Then she noticed the slight incline of his head toward the living room. "Oh, *that* door. Of course."

Charlotte dropped the hot pad on the counter and led the way through the dimly-lit dining room and into the hall. She could feel Mac's presence close behind her.

Near the front door she reached to flick on the light, but Mac's hand stopped her.

He didn't say anything for a moment, just absently played with her fingers. Then his eyes sought hers in the grainy darkness. "Do you mind me stopping by like this? I probably should have called."

Charlotte shook her head, wondering why he hadn't phoned a few days ago. "It looks as if you survived the replay of the Spanish Inquisition."

"No problem," he chuckled. "She's trying to protect you from those of us who'd lead you astray." His fingers intertwined with hers.

"My mother doesn't seem to think I can take care of myself."

"She must not know you very well."

Charlotte smiled, pleased by his faith in her abilities. Then another thought hit her. "I hope you don't think I told her we were dating."

"I don't."

"Because I didn't." Charlotte ignored his denial. "I wouldn't tell her that."

"Charlotte, I never once thought you did. You won't even admit it to yourself." He didn't add that he'd resisted thinking in those terms himself. Not calling her had been his own form of denial. He moved closer, sandwiching her between himself and the wall.

"But it's not—" His lips brushed across hers, interrupting her words. "True."

"Then maybe we should remedy that." Mac ignored the voice of reason that had been advising him to back off and give both of them a little breathing room. He pressed against her softness, feeling the heat of her breasts through his sweater. Backing off was the last thing he had in mind.

Mac's teeth nipped at her ear lobe, his breath

warmed it. "I'll be back from Washington Sunday. Have dinner with me."

"I can't." Her head fell to one side, allowing his marauding mouth greater access to her neck. "My mother will be here."

"When's she leaving?" His chin nudged away her shirt collar and he traced her collar bone with his tongue.

Charlotte sagged against the wall. "Monday."

"Monday night then?" His breath sent goose bumps dancing across her damp skin.

Charlotte shook her head, nearly moaning in frustration. "I have to work."

Raising his head, his eyes skewered hers in the shaft of moonlight that slanted through the window. "When?"

"Friday."

Now it was Mac's turn to groan. "Over a week away. I don't know if I can make it." His mouth ground down, forcing her pliant lips apart.

Charlotte's tongue met his, her arms wrapped around his narrow waist and she wondered what in the world had taken possession of her common sense. This might be a first date she'd agreed upon, but they were far beyond the hand holding stage. His arousal pressed penetratingly hard against her stomach, and she rubbed wantonly against it, unmindful of her mother and teenage daughter sitting in the kitchen.

Reason told her that she'd just agreed to more than a date. The thought, though wildly exciting, scared her. Had she agreed to have an affair with him? Charlotte Handley just wasn't the type to engage in illicit intrigues. But somehow she thought he'd ex-

pect more Friday night than a burger and a good
night kiss. But an affair? Still, what else was there?
Marriage? Oh, no! Brian had taught her an unforget-
table lesson concerning that fine institution. Besides,
Mac certainly hadn't proposed.

He was thinking affair. She'd bet on it. But what
would he do when he found out she was frigid? With
more presence of mind than she felt, Charlotte wedged
her hands between their bodies and pushed. Instantly,
his heat and support withdrew and Charlotte grabbed
hold of his arms to keep from falling. The kiss took
longer to end. With a leisurely pace that sent currents
of desire through Charlotte, their lips separated.

"I'm sorry, sweetheart." He still leaned toward
her, but now only their foreheads touched. "I forgot
we weren't alone."

As if on cue, Ida Smith's voice carried from the
kitchen. "You all right, Charlotte?"

Charlotte tried to answer but laughter bubbled up
in her throat. At the sound of her mother's voice,
Mac had jerked away from her like a kid caught with
his hand in the cookie jar.

"Charlotte?"

"Yes, mother, I'm fine." Charlotte bit her bottom
lip to keep from giggling.

"You're sure?" The scratching of chair legs against
linoleum accompanied the question.

"Mother! I'll be there in a minute. Save me some
brownies." That seemed to satisfy her, at least Charlotte didn't hear any more activity from the kitchen.

Charlotte looked over at Mac. He stood, bracing
his shoulder against the door, and she could tell by
the quaking of his body that he was trying to stifle his

laughter. She threw her hands up in defeat feeling utterly foolish. "Mac, I—"

"Ssshhh." He gathered her up in his arms, pressing two fingers to her lips.

Unlike before, when his embrace had been wildly exciting, now it seemed gentle and comforting. Charlotte rested her cheek against the prickly wool sweater.

"I haven't felt like this since I tried stealing kisses from Annabelle Dameron at the ripe old age of fourteen."

"Oh, Mac. I'm so embarrassed."

"Don't be." He put his hands on her shoulders and held her out at arm's length, so he could see her face. In the dim light Charlotte noticed the mirth gleaming in his eyes. "I always thought stealing kisses great fun. But, Charlotte, I have to tell you, Annabelle couldn't hold a candle to you."

Heat spread through her, staining her cheeks. Mac smoothed out her shirt, refolding her collar before looking back into her eyes. No laughter remained in his gaze as his hand slid down the rumpled flannel to cup her breast. "I better go."

Charlotte nodded. "About Friday night." This seemed as good a time as any to back out.

"What about it?" His thumb flicked her nipple and the sensitive point pressed against the flannel.

"Mmmm." Charlotte's eyes drifted shut. "What time should I be ready?" So much for backing out.

"I'll call you Sunday night." His hand dropped to his side, and Mac quickly kissed the tip of her nose. "I *really* better go. Happy Thanksgiving."

Charlotte stepped out onto the porch, unmindful of the cold, and watched him jog around the corner of the house. Moments later, the Jeep's engine roared to life, and Mac backed out of her driveway and turned onto the street. His taillights were disappearing into the darkness when Charlotte heard her mother.

"Charlotte? Charlotte, honey, what are you doing? I thought I felt a draft."

Sighing in resignation, Charlotte stepped into the hall and closed the door behind her. She squinted against the brightness of the light her mother had turned on.

"Charlotte, you're going to catch your death going outside in this weather without a coat."

"I'm fine." Charlotte realized she was rubbing her arms and stopped regardless of the chills that ran through her.

"Why I just can't imagine what got into that Mr. McQuade's mind to take you out of the house like that."

"He didn't take me out, I stepped onto the porch on my own."

Ida's expression conveyed disbelief. "Well, I say you wouldn't go leaving the door open if you knew how much oil cost."

"But I do."

"What?" Her mother stopped walking toward the kitchen and turned. "What did you say, Charlotte?"

"I do know how much oil costs, and electricity, and gas, and a mortgage. I know because I pay them."

"Of course you do, dear. It's just that I know you're used to so much and you won't take any money from Brian, and well, I worry about you."

"Oh, Mom." Charlotte took her mother's hand in

hers, noticing the calluses that years of hard work had produced, as she led her into the living room. "Sit down."

Charlotte sank onto the couch beside her mother. "I don't want you worrying about me. I keep telling you that Elizabeth and I are doing fine."

"But you always say that. Even when you were a little girl and I knew you'd bitten off more than you could chew, you'd never ask for help."

"Mom." Charlotte bent forward and hugged the older woman. "This time it's true. I have to budget my money, but I do have enough—and some of it's from Brian." She saw her mother's surprise and went on. "I said I wouldn't live on his charity anymore, but he does provide child support for Elizabeth. And he pays my college expenses, plus I have the money from the sale of the house in Richmond. Besides that, there's my job at the library. So you see, we're hardly destitute."

"But, Charlotte, you gave up so much."

Charlotte shook her head realizing that nothing she could say would change her mother's mind, but she tried anyway. "I'm happy now, Mother. And I'm doing what I wanted to do from the beginning."

"But—"

"Hey, isn't anyone going to help me eat these brownies? I made them for you guys," Elizabeth's voice interrupted from the next room.

"Coming, Lizzy." Charlotte stood up, offering Ida her hand. "Let's go indulge ourselves with chocolate."

The visit had actually gone by quickly, Charlotte thought as she stood at the bus depot waving to her mother. Charlotte had even suggested that Ida stay out the week, but her mother had been anxious to get back to more familiar surroundings.

Charlotte knew better than to think her mother was convinced that divorcing Brian had been a good idea; but after the evening of their talk, Ida had kept her comments on the subject to a minimum.

Of course, she still had plenty to say, especially after Charlotte hung up the phone Sunday evening.

"Was that him?" she'd demanded before Charlotte had even cradled the receiver.

"If you're referring to Mac McQuade, then, yes, it was." Charlotte had tried to give her mother a "let's drop the subject" look, but to no avail. Charlotte wanted to go off by herself and allow her heart rate to return to normal. It had inexplicably sped up the moment she'd heard Mac's voice.

"What did he want?"

Charlotte continued dicing the left-over turkey. "He just called to tell me he was home," she lied. Better to tell her that than what they'd really talked about— their date for Friday night. Actually, Mac had talked; Charlotte had listened, adding only a single word comment to the conversation every now and then.

"Oh, so he checks in with you. This sounds serious."

The knife clattered onto the chopping block and Charlotte put her hands on her hips. "Mother! He does not check in with me, and it is *not* serious."

Ida had been undaunted. "Well, you're the one that said he called to tell you he was home. Is he coming over this evening?"

"No." She'd resumed fragmenting the turkey.

"Why not?"

"I have no idea." *I told him not to.*

"Too bad. He seems like such a nice young man. If you two were to get married then you wouldn't have to work so hard."

"Mother." Charlotte had given up on the turkey that now looked more shredded than diced. "*If* I were to marry again," she'd said, wondering when her never had been downgraded to if, "it wouldn't be so that some man could take care of me. I can do that myself."

After that her mother had changed the subject, before wandering out of the room to find Elizabeth, leaving Charlotte alone with her thoughts.

Now as she watched her mother's bus pull away in a cloud of foul-smelling exhaust, those same disturbing thoughts haunted Charlotte. What was she going to do about Friday night?

Should she go with him to one of the taverns for dinner and then to Chownings for The Gambol like he'd suggested on the phone, or what? Break their date? She'd certainly given him no indication that she considered that action and time was running out. Charlotte glanced at her watch.

Now look what all this thinking had gotten her. She was going to have to hurry or be late for her job. Mrs. Helm, the head librarian, had increased Charlotte's hours as a favor to her and being tardy was no way to repay her.

Fifteen minutes later Charlotte sat behind her desk in the library's research section. She'd just called Elizabeth, telling her to warm up some turkey for her dinner. Her daughter had agreed, but only after extracting a promise from Charlotte that tomorrow night they'd have pizza—the kind with pepperoni, not turkey. Charlotte shook her head. Maybe she had been pushing Tom Turkey a bit too much lately. When she got home from work, she'd freeze the rest of the leftovers.

"Excuse me. I was told you were the person to see." The excitingly familiar voice interrupted Charlotte's fowl thoughts.

Her head shot up, and the pencil she'd used to write a note to herself clattered to the blotter then rolled to the floor. "What are you doing here?"

"I didn't know you wore glasses." Mac grinned down into Charlotte's startled face before bending down and retrieving her pencil.

"Just for reading." Charlotte whipped off the horn-rimmed glasses she'd always thought made her look bookish.

"I like them." Mac handed her the pencil. "They fit the image. You know, staid librarian."

"Thanks." Charlotte grabbed the pencil and jammed it into a cup filled with writing instruments.

"You're welcome." Mac leaned his hip against the desk. "Seeing you with glasses reminds me of a movie I saw once. There was this prim little lady who everyone thought was as quiet and retiring as a church mouse."

Mac paused, picked up a framed photograph of Elizabeth and examined it. "Nice picture. The photographer did a great job of catching her exuberance." His eyes met hers. "You take it?"

Charlotte nodded, wondering why all he had to do was look at her, and she felt all warm and mushy inside.

"Thought so." He replaced the picture beside the bud vase holding one sorry looking white rose. He'd have to buy her some more, so she could throw this one out.

"Well, anyway, this lady in the movie—she taught school instead of working in a library—had everyone, including the leading man, thinking her wallflower material. Then one day she lets down her hair." Mac reached across the desk and brushed a curly tendril behind Charlotte's ear. "She wore it in some sort of little knot on her head. And zapps off her glasses and . . . you can imagine what happened next."

Mac's devilish wink sent Charlotte's imagination soaring. Needless to say, she found herself typecast perfectly as the prim schoolmarm turned librarian, and there could only be one leading man. Charlotte blinked as the scenes ran through her mind, rapidly slipping in rating from PG to X. Charlotte swallowed and tried to pull herself back together.

What if Mrs. Helm saw her? Although she'd never seen it addressed specifically, Charlotte felt confident that librarians weren't suppose to engage in erotic daydreams with sexy men draped across their desks. "What?" Charlotte began and stopped. Realizing her voice sounded too loud for her surroundings, she lowered it to a stage whisper and started again. "What are you doing here? I'm working."

"I know. There's some information I need help in finding."

Charlotte could tell when he even thought about smiling, before his lips so much as moved. She wondered if he knew what a dead giveaway those dimples were. Right now they told her that he didn't have heavy duty research on his mind—at least not the kind you find in books.

Mac assessed the doubtful expression on Charlotte's face and raised his hands in submission. "Honest."

"Well, you'll have to get another librarian to help you. I'm busy." Charlotte indicated the book on her desk that she'd been searching for the name of an act passed by parliament to restrict privateering.

"It won't take long."

"Perhaps you could find the information yourself then?"

He shook his head. "Libraries intimidate me."

Charlotte gave him a look that clearly stated she didn't buy that for one second. Frankly, she'd be surprised if *anything* intimidated him. "Oh, all right. What do you need?"

There was that smile she knew had been lurking below the surface. Mac stuffed his hand down the front pocket of his jeans and pulled out a slip of paper. With an I-told-you-so flourish, he handed it to Charlotte.

She did her best to ignore the warmth of the paper as she opened it. Lord knows she tried not to think about how close it had been to part of his anatomy. Her eyes scanned the writing, and she bit her bottom lip to keep from laughing. "Don't forget to pick it up Thursday."

"What?"

"Your navy blazer." Charlotte handed him the paper. "You gave me a dry cleaner's receipt."

Mac had the decency to look sheepish as he took the receipt. "Must be in the other pocket."

"Listen, Mac—"

"No, I think I found it." His hand had disappeared into his jeans pocket, and Charlotte had to stop herself from offering to help search for the missing paper. "Here it is." He held out his hand, thought better of it, and examined the paper himself. Satisfied, he placed it on her desk.

"It's a quote from a song written in the eighteenth century." Mac had scribbled it down before leaving his house. "I thought I might use it in a lesson."

"And you need to know . . ."

"Who wrote it and what it's called."

Charlotte read the line. She'd heard it before, but couldn't place the source. "Okay, let me see if I can find it." Somehow she wasn't surprised when he started to follow her down the book-lined aisle. Telling herself she needed them, Charlotte backtracked, picked up her glasses and put them on.

"You're good at this." Mac leaned against a bookshelf watching Charlotte climb down a step stool. She'd looked through several resource books, each time getting closer to finding the information she sought.

"Thanks." She flipped to the index. "It's what I've always wanted to do."

"Really?"

"Sure." Charlotte looked up, pushing her glasses back into place with her finger. "That's my major, library science."

"Is this what you like to do? Research?"

"I'm not certain. The research is really interesting. I'm always learning new things. For example, that line of yours is from 'Heart of Oak' written in 1759 by David Garrick." She showed him the reference to it in the book. "But I also enjoy working with children. So at this point, I'm not certain."

"You're good with children. I mean, you and Elizabeth seem to have a great relationship." Mac jotted down the information, noting that it matched what he had at home. He felt the tiniest bit guilty about deceiving her, but he'd had an overwhelming desire to see her, and this *had* seemed preferable to a commando style attack on her house.

"Thank you. We've always been close." Charlotte closed the book, but allowed Mac to return the volume to its spot on the top shelf.

"Elizabeth doesn't mention her father much." Mac climbed down from the step stool. "Does she see him often?" He turned to face her, knowing his question strained the boundaries of their relationship, willing her to answer it and break those confines.

"Occasionally." Charlotte traced the gold lettering on a book's spine, refusing to meet his blue-green gaze. "Brian didn't really want children." She lost the battle and looked up. "He expresses little desire to have her visit."

Mac shook his head, wondering what kind of man would pass up a chance to be around a kid like Elizabeth. He gazed into Charlotte's clear blue eyes and his heart beat faster. Obviously this Brian was a first rate moron. Not fighting like the devil to keep a woman like Charlotte was proof enough of that. Then Mac remembered they were discussing the man's daughter, not his ex-wife. "How does Elizabeth feel about it?"

Charlotte shifted her weight from one foot to the other. Surrounded by row upon row of books, the two of them were cocooned by the written word. For a moment, it seemed as if no one else existed. Yet other people did exist. "Elizabeth tries to act as if it doesn't bother her, but I think it does. It must." Charlotte began leading the way back toward her desk. "She does things now and again that convince me that she misses having a father."

"Like what?"

"Like . . ." Charlotte waved her hand in dismissal. "Just silly things. You know kids." Had she almost blurted out what she really believed? That Elizabeth did everything possible to promote a friendship between her mother and what she considered a very likely father substitute, her teacher, Mr. McQuade. But just because Elizabeth considered someone a ready-made papa, didn't make it so.

Besides, when Mac stared at her the way he did right now, Charlotte didn't think playing daddy was upper most in his mind. Charlotte sat behind her desk and began shuffling through the papers littering the top. When she began to feel foolish, Charlotte looked up. Mac's gaze hadn't wavered. Flustered, Charlotte folded her hands, hoping he'd leave. After all, how could she be expected to do her job with *him* standing so close. "Is there anything else I can do for you?"

Charlotte knew even before she noticed the decidedly wicked gleam in his eye, that Mac's interpretation of her question differed from her original intent. She laced her fingers to still their wringing motion. How could she feel so comfortable with him one moment and so disconcerted the next?

Mac grinned and reached for the jacket he'd left draped across a chair. "No, nothing else . . . at the moment. Thanks for the information." He patted his front jeans pocket where he'd stuffed the folded piece of paper.

"Of course. It's my job." Had he noticed her eyes following the movement of his hand? Was her face as red as her hair?

He shrugged into the bomber jacket. "Is seven o'clock all right for me to pick you up on Friday?"

Tell him you're not going. Tell him you recognize that wolf-stalking-the-lamb expression, and you have no intention of becoming mutton chops. "Seven will be fine."

"You're certain?"

"Of course." There was nothing to worry about. They'd go out, have a good time; and when he brought her back to her house, they'd share a few kisses. Well, maybe a little more than a few, but after all, Elizabeth their unwitting chaperone, would be there. What did Charlotte have to worry about?

"You worry too much. That's my job."

Mac grimaced at the telephone. It had been ringing when he'd walked in the door, and as soon as he'd answered it and heard Sid Green's voice, he'd known he was in for a lecture. His agent wasn't disappointing him.

"Are you there, Benjamin?"

Mac sighed. Sid was one of the few people who still called him by his given name. Mac guessed it had a lot to do with the fact that the agent had helped make Benjamin McQuade a recognized name in literary circles.

"Benjamin?"

"Yeah, I'm here, Sid. But like I told you. The book needs more work." There was a pause on the other end of the line, and Mac could picture Sid in his plush, uptown office, running his fingers through his nearly nonexistent hair.

"So, how long have we known each other, Benjamin?"

"A while." Mac strode across the room and sank onto the couch. He might as well get comfortable for this.

"Forever, Benjamin. I've known you forever. I knew you before you went off to that God awful war, before you wrote your first book, even before you grew into that ugly mug of yours that most women can't seem to resist. You were nothing but a snaggle-toothed kid that first time your father brought you into town to meet me. Remember?"

Mac smiled at the memory. "Sure, Sid."

"But do you recall what you said to me that day?"

"Sid this doesn't change anything."

"You said, 'Mr. Green, I'm going to be a writer.' And I thought to myself, Sid, this kid's got chutzpah. It took a couple years till I found out that you had the talent to go with it."

Mac shifted against the pillows. "How's Dolores?"

"Don't try to change the subject on me, Benjamin. My wife is fine as you well know. She told me she sent you a letter last week. What I want to know is what happened to that boy who wanted to write?"

"Sid, I'm not ready."

"Okay. Never let it be said that Sid Green pushes his clients, let alone his friends." He seemed to ignore Mac's bark of laughter. "But let me ask you this. Have you been to the movies lately? The time is ripe for a good book on Vietnam. And more important." His voice softened. "I think you're ready to let go of this part of your past."

Mac pushed the antenna into the phone and leaned over the arm of the couch to set it on the table. He'd spent the last twenty minutes trying to convince Sid that he wasn't holding onto his past—that the manuscript just wasn't ready for publication. But Mac didn't think his old friend Sid was fooled, and worse, neither was Mac.

Mac stretched out and stacked his hands under his head. His counselor at the V.A. hospital had a long, fancy name for his malady, but at the moment, Mac couldn't remember what it was. Sid had hit it pretty close to the mark though. Being a P.O.W had taught him to hold on tight to a lot of things, Mac thought, and he had learned the lesson well, maybe too well.

Sharing himself with others was what he needed to do. Opening up his past, his future, his dreams . . . his fears. Mac ran his fingers through his hair. Hadn't he done his part? He'd written the damn book, hadn't he?

Mac jumped to his feet and jerked off his jacket. With an impatient motion, he threw it on the couch and paced to the window. The sight of filtered moonlight dancing on the river did nothing to soothe his mood.

All right, he'd admit it. It wasn't the book that bothered him, or even Sid. It was Charlotte. Mac rested his forehead against the cold glass. He had a sneaking suspicion that he was falling in love with her. And part of him was scared to death. Loving Charlotte would mean sharing—and he had yet to tell her one blessed thing about himself.

EIGHT

". . . and Ali wants me to spend the night, so we can get an early start horseback riding."

"That's nice, Lizzy. Could we talk about it later? I really need to finish typing this paper." Charlotte tried to find her place on the margin-filled, hand-scribbled sheet that she and Sally Reinert had written.

"It's all right then? I mean if I stay over tonight?"

"Sure, honey." Charlotte hit the j instead of the h, mumbling a curse as she backspaced and stuck correction tape into the ancient portable typewriter. She never should have agreed to type the paper. Why had she told Sally it would be ready for proofreading this weekend? There was just too much going on today. First there was her date with Mac, then Elizabeth had said something about spending the night at Ali's. . . .

Charlotte's hands froze on the keys.

"Elizabeth! Elizabeth!" Charlotte's voice began as a panicked shriek and grew louder.

"What's wrong, Mom?" Elizabeth almost skidded to a stop in front of the card table set up in her mother's room.

"Did you say something earlier about spending the night at Allison's?"

"Yeah. You said I could."

"Well, you can't."

"But, Mom! How come?"

Charlotte stared at her daughter's upset face a moment without answering. What could she say? Elizabeth dear, I'm afraid if you aren't here, your teacher and I will fall into each other's arms and make passionate love. No. That was no good. As a matter of fact, she couldn't think of *any* response that made sense.

"Why can't I, Mom?"

"Shopping. Yes, I thought we might do some Christmas shopping Saturday morning." Charlotte let out a sigh of relief, thankful for the inspiration. "We could get an early start. Even drive to Hampton—or Richmond."

"Well, gee, Mom." Elizabeth plopped down on Charlotte's bed. "That sounds great, but Ali already called the stables. I asked you last week if we could go riding this weekend and you said yes."

Charlotte rubbed the back of her neck. "That's right, I did."

"I guess I could call Ali and cancel. . . ."

"No." Charlotte shook her head. "No. You go on with Allison. I know how you've been looking forward to this."

"Are you sure?"

"Yes. You go and have a good time." Charlotte

held out her arms, giving Elizabeth a hard squeeze when she stepped into them. "We can fight the crowds next weekend. I'll probably still be typing this tomorrow, anyway. And, Elizabeth. It's all right with me if you spend the night at Ali's." She could hardly expect her fourteen year old daughter to be the guardian of her mother's virtue.

Besides, though she hated to admit it, Charlotte wondered if she truly wanted her virtue guarded. Ever since the thought of making love with Mac had entered her mind, it had been doing strange things to her imagination. Fantasies she'd never thought herself capable of swam around in her head.

They weren't just sexual fantasies, although there were certainly plenty of those. Charlotte found herself imagining all sorts of things. At times, in her mind, she and Mac would be walking hand in hand along a beach or watching the sun rise over the York River. Or they'd be spending quiet evenings at home watching television with Elizabeth. Today, she even imagined herself having Mac's baby. When that gem had flashed into her thoughts, Charlotte realized she'd fallen in love with Mac.

"Hey, Mom. Isn't Mr. McQuade picking you up at seven?"

Elizabeth's question jolted Charlotte's mind away from its wondrous discovery. "Uh, yes." Charlotte tried to find her place on the paper again.

"Well, that's less than an hour away."

"Oh no," Charlotte moaned, glancing at her watch. "I'll never get this finished."

"Don't worry about it, Mom."

"But Sally is expecting—"

Elizabeth gently, but firmly, pushed Charlotte from the chair. "I'll do it."

"But—"

"Hey, I can type." Elizabeth feigned indignation.

"I know you can, Lizzy. But what about Allison?"

Elizabeth settled onto the chair. "Her mom's not picking me up till seven thirty, and I'm ready except for throwing a few things in my duffle bag. Besides," Elizabeth gave her mother a cheeky grin, "I'm not going on a date with hunky Mr. McQuade."

Charlotte laughed in spite of herself. "You better watch it, young lady, or I'll tell Mr. McQuade what you call him. Then he'll stick you in a corner with a dunce cap on your head."

Charlotte was just picking up her new bottle of perfume when the door bell rang. Daringly, at least to her way of thinking, she unbuttoned her silk dress and sprayed the flowery scent between her breasts. The atomized droplets cooled her skin and Charlotte felt her nipples tighten in response.

"Mom! Mr. McQuade is here."

Charlotte guiltily fastened the shirt top dress up to her neck, thought better of it and undid the top two buttons. "I'll be right there."

Mac and Elizabeth were sitting on the sofa discussing the high school basketball team's chances for a winning season when Charlotte walked into the living room. Seeing them together reminded her of the fantasy about her family watching T.V. They didn't notice her at first and she stood watching them talk and laugh together.

"There you are, Mom," At Elizabeth's words, Mac turned. He smiled at Charlotte, and she felt bathed in a warm golden glow. He stood, walked around the couch, and handed Charlotte a single white rose wrapped in green tissue.

"For your desk at the library."

"Thank you." Charlotte smelled the blossom, but her gaze never left Mac. His charcoal grey suit and white shirt were finely tailored and fit his broad-shouldered body perfectly. Yet, beneath his polished exterior, Charlotte sensed something wild and un-tamed about him. Maybe it was the strand of sun-streaked brown hair that the wind had blown across his forehead. Charlotte had an almost uncontrollable urge to reach out and brush it back.

"How about if I put it in some water?" Elizabeth took the flower, and Charlotte wondered how long she'd been standing there letting her eyes wander over Mac. She would definitely have to watch herself.

"Thanks, Lizzy."

When Elizabeth disappeared into the kitchen, Mac leaned toward Charlotte. "You look lovely tonight."

Charlotte glanced up and saw herself reflected in his aquamarine eyes. She'd never felt more beautiful.

"There." Elizabeth came back into the room and set the vase down on the coffee table. Charlotte and Mac each searched for something to stare at besides one another.

"Our reservations are for seven fifteen."

"Oh, then we should go." Charlotte hurried into the hall to get her coat. When she carried it back into the living room, she overheard Mac ask Elizabeth if she would like to come along.

"Gee, that's nice, Mr. McQuade, but I'm going to

spend the night at Allison's house. We're going horse-back riding tomorrow.''

Charlotte tried to tell herself that she imagined Mac's heated glance when Elizabeth mentioned her sleeping arrangements for the night. But she couldn't ignore the shiver of excitement that ricocheted through her body.

''Do you have all your things ready, Lizzy?'' Charlotte attempted to sound like a competent mother rather than a woman anticipating a rendezvous with her lover.

''Sure, Mom, and I put your paper in the mailbox for Mrs. Reinert.''

''Thanks, honey.'' Charlotte brushed a red curl off her daughter's forehead. ''Have a good time, but be careful on those horses.''

''Aw, Mom. I used to go riding every weekend. You don't have to worry about me.''

''Yes, but I do. Besides, it's been a long time since you were on a horse. Remember that.''

''M-o-m!''

Charlotte threw up her hands. ''All right. Just be careful.''

After the warmth of the house, the night seemed sharp, almost brittle. Charlotte and Mac hurried to the shelter of his car. Mac had no sooner shut the door behind him when he reached across the gear shift, gently clutched Charlotte's coat lapels, and dragged her toward him. Though his face and lips were cold from the air, when he opened his mouth and his warm tongue caressed hers, Charlotte forgot all about the weather.

The kiss lasted just long enough for Charlotte to

wish the stick shift and all the bulky clothes that separated them would disappear.

"Sorry." Mac's breath fanned her cheek. "I couldn't wait any longer to do that."

"It's all right." Charlotte's voice was a sensual whisper. At least it must have sounded that way to Mac because in less than a heartbeat his lips were again pressed against hers.

Mac forced himself to pull away with a self-deprecating laugh. "When was the last time you were ravished in the front seat of a Jeep, Mrs. Handley?"

"I don't recall it ever happening."

"Well, I better get this thing moving or you're going to be in for a new, and considering the layout of the seats, uncomfortable experience."

Mac turned the key and the engine grumbled to life. "What's this?" Mac reached across Charlotte, opened the glove compartment and took out a tissue. "Something has steamed the windshield up so much that I can't see."

Charlotte couldn't help laughing when he bobbed his eyebrows and leered at her. What was happening to her? They were sharing passionate kisses, talking, even joking about them, and she wasn't the slightest bit embarrassed.

They walked hand in gloved hand from the parking lot to King's Arms Tavern. The small-paned windows reflected welcoming candlelight much as they must have in 1752 when Mrs. Jane Vobe first opened the establishment. A waiter in colonial garb seated them at a small, cozy table near a roaring fireplace.

"Too warm?" Mac looked across the table at

Charlotte. The golden glow of candles and burning logs set off dancing sparks of fire in her hair. He could barely resist the urge to reach out and be consumed by her heat.

"No. It feels good after being outside. Are you?"

Mac swallowed and shook his head, not trusting himself to speak.

"Everything looks so wonderful." Charlotte dragged her eyes away from Mac's gaze and pretended to study the bill of fare. If she looked at the naked desire in his expression any longer, she'd shock them both by suggesting they skip dinner and race back to her house.

"What would you like?"

Charlotte knew he was asking about dinner—she did. Then why did her mind keep conjuring up more erotic visions than Cornish game hen? "I don't know. I've never eaten here before."

"You haven't?" Small talk about food helped keep his mind off the fact that Charlotte would be spending the night alone—at least her daughter wouldn't be there.

"No." Charlotte glanced down at the prices. "I'm afraid this menu is designed for wealthier people than I."

"You have something against folks with money?"

Charlotte looked up from the Sally Lunn bread she was buttering. "Did I sound resentful?"

"A little."

"I didn't mean to. I have nothing against money per say. It's just the importance some people place on having it and the power they can wield against others that bothers me."

Mac studied Charlotte over the rim of his water glass. "Are we talking about your former husband here?"

Charlotte's eyes met his for an instant, then skittered away.

"You told me once he was rich," Mac continued. "I gathered at the time that bothered you."

"I never realized my feelings were so transparent."

"They aren't. I just make a practice of examining you—and your feelings."

Charlotte shook her head and smiled. "I'll have to remember that. Anyway, my prejudices against the wealthy shouldn't affect you. No offense, but teacher's salaries are hardly a state secret." As soon as the words passed her lips, Charlotte wished she could pull them back. How could she say such a thing to him?

"Ah, so you like me for my poverty." Mac's stomach tightened as he thought about the trust fund that multiplied even as they sat pondering what to eat. Money begat money. He really should tell her.

"I like you for a lot of reasons," Charlotte said. He didn't seem to be offended by her thoughtless remark. "Not being loaded down with money is just one of them."

Mac reasoned that she'd said that only because she thought him a man of limited means—at least that's what he hoped. After all, he didn't flaunt his money or try to manipulate people with it. But as Mac ate his ramekin of oysters, he still worried about it, and wondered why he didn't just tell her.

"Would you like some dessert?" The waitress had

cleared away the dishes, and Mac had taken Charlotte's hand in his own.

"No, thank you."

"I can afford it, if you want something." Mac had meant his remark to be funny but he could tell by her expression and the way she gripped his thumb that she didn't think it was.

"Oh, I knew it," Charlotte said, her eyes searching his. "I hurt your feelings with that remark about your salary? Please forgive me. You know I think you're a wonderful teacher, and I truly respect what you do, and—"

"Charlotte. It's okay. My feelings aren't hurt. My pride's intact. It was a stupid joke on my part. Now would you like some dessert? Their pecan pie is great."

Charlotte's hand relaxed in his. "No thanks. I really don't think I could eat another bite."

They walked the short distance down Duke of Gloucester Street to Chowning's Tavern. The crowd in the eighteenth century alehouse was louder and more jovial than the group they'd just left. Mac found them a seat in the corner and ordered draft beer for himself and cider, mulled and spiced, for Charlotte.

"What are we going to do?" Charlotte asked as she noticed men in flowing shirts and breeches setting up tables with oversize cards and dice.

"You'll see." Mac smiled across the rough-hewn table at her. "Have you ever played Goose?"

"No. Have you?"

"Once or twice, but I don't think experience is necessary."

An hour later the crowd had grown even larger. She and Mac had listened to ballads sung by roving troubadours, had tried their luck at cards and a game of chance called Loo. They'd even tossed the dice in Goose.

"Would you like some more cider?" Mac eyed the empty mug that seemed to have Charlotte's undivided attention.

"No." Charlotte looked up. "Thanks, but I think three glasses is my limit."

"Can't hold your cider, huh?" He grinned.

"I guess not. But if you want something else, go ahead."

Mac shook his head. "I'm driving."

Charlotte looked back at her mug.

Mac stared at the top of her burnished head, longing to sink his fingers into the bright red curls. Instead he reached out and lifted her chin. "Bored?"

"Oh no, I've had a wonderful time this evening."

"But not now."

Charlotte gazed into his eyes, wondering what to say. Every fiber of her being was aware of him, every sense inundated. And every second that ticked off the high case clock in the corner made her more conscious of the fact that she wanted him. If only she could shake the nagging doubts about being able to please him.

"Charlotte?"

Concern laced his voice and Charlotte wet her suddenly dry lips. "Do you suppose we could leave?"

"Of course." Mac stood and pulled out her chair. "Are you ill?"

"No." The word escaped with a nervous laugh. *Charlotte Handley you are not good at this.* She was trying to entice a man back to her empty house, and he thought she was sick.

Mac paid the bill, helped Charlotte on with her coat and hustled them outside, never once changing the worried expression on his face. When he tried to all but lift her down Chowning's front porch steps, Charlotte balked.

"Would you stop treating me like I'm going to faint, or worse yet, get sick all over you?"

Mac let go of her arm as if she'd slapped him. He stared up at her from the sidewalk. "Fine. But would you like to explain to me why you all of a sudden got white as a sheet and wanted to leave?"

For an intelligent man he could be very dense. "I have no idea why I'm pale, except maybe because I'm not used to this and I'm nervous."

Mac ran his hand through his hair. "Nervous about what?"

Oh, for heaven's sake. How did she get into this conversation? And how could she get out? Charlotte started to turn away. Mac's hands reached out and grabbed her shoulders.

"Nervous about what?" he repeated.

"About asking you to come back to my house with me," Charlotte blurted out.

His dimples signaled the beginnings of a smile, and soon his entire face sported a decidedly wicked grin. "Is that what this is all about?"

Charlotte bit her lip and nodded.

"You want to go back to your house—your empty house with me?" Mac couldn't help teasing her. She'd really worried him inside. He *had* thought she was going to faint.

Was he trying to be cute?

"Why didn't you just say so?"

"I thought I did." Charlotte tried to squirm out of his grasp as the tavern door opened and a group of patrons left, but he wouldn't let go.

"Charlotte?"

She'd looked away when the people had walked by, but now the magnetism of his voice pulled her gaze back to his. "What?"

"I haven't been able to think of anything but taking you back to that empty house all evening."

"You haven't?" Charlotte still stood on the porch and the added height put them on eye level.

"No, but I didn't want to push you. Next time maybe we should devise a signal. You could kick me under the table."

Charlotte laughed, not telling him that she thought his plan could be dangerous. If she were to kick him every time she had the urge to get him alone, he'd have permanently bruised shins.

"I still don't want to push you." Why in the hell was he being so gallant?

"You're not."

"Oh, Charlotte, I want you so damn much."

Before Charlotte knew what was happening, his hands curved around her neck, and she was being thoroughly kissed—right there on Duke of Gloucester Street. She thought her repertoire of fantasies was fairly complete, but she'd never imagined this.

"Must be newlyweds." The words spoken very close to her ear made Charlotte jump away from Mac. She looked straight into the face of an elderly woman she'd noticed in the game room. The woman's smile was sweet as she linked her arm through her companion's and climbed down the stairs, but Charlotte was embarrassed.

"Come on." Mac grabbed her hand and headed for the parking lot.

Neither of them spoke on the short ride back to Charlotte's house. The porch light was on, and Elizabeth had left a note on the hall table telling Charlotte she'd be home around four o'clock the next day.

"Elizabeth's at her friend's house." Charlotte dropped the note on the table and turned toward Mac.

"So I gathered." Mac moved closer. "Listen, Charlotte, you've got to know how much I want you, but like I said earlier, I don't want to push." He shrugged. "If you're not sure. . . ."

"I am!" Charlotte clutched his arm, realized what she'd done, and let her hand drop. He wasn't going to leave, was he? "I want you to stay. It's just . . . well, I'm not used to this."

"If it helps any, I should say that I'm not exactly used to this either." Mac started at the neck and pushed the buttons of Charlotte's coat through the holes, one by one.

"You're not?" Charlotte asked in disbelief.

When she looked at him with those big blue eyes, she reminded him of a sweet innocent, her teenage daughter not withstanding. He felt jaded in comparison. "I've probably had more experience than you," he admitted honestly. "But I don't start love affairs every day."

"That's what we're doing, isn't it?" Charlotte's heart beat erratically as he slid the coat down her arms.

"It has all the earmarks."

Whispered against the tender flesh beneath her jaw his words were wildly arousing. Charlotte had known for sometime—maybe since the first moment she'd seen him in that silly fish tie—that their relationship would come to this. Still, a tiny part of her wished for something more. "Newlyweds," the grandmotherly lady had said. Is that what was missing? A wedding? But that would mean marriage, and Charlotte certainly didn't want that. Did she?

The decision to eliminate such weighty thoughts from her mind was not a conscious one—it just happened. One second she was contemplating whether or not she wanted to marry Mac, and the next she wondered what was the quickest way to get him undressed.

"Hmmm, you smell good."

His chin, the raspy whiskers sending chills down her spine, forged a path down the V of her neck line. "It's new perfume."

"I like it."

She'd thought he would when she'd first caught a whiff of it in the store. The scent had evoked visions of bodies—their bodies—naked and shimmering in the sun, entwined on a sea of wildflowers. The fantasy struck her now with such force that her legs grew weak, her knees almost crumbling.

As if he knew of her dilemma, Mac scooped her into his arms, pressing her against his thundering heart. "I'm not a patient man, Charlotte," he said and carried her down the hall. He peeked in Elizabeth's bedroom first, dismissed it as not belonging to Charlotte, and entered the other bedroom.

In a slow, sensual way that belied his earlier words, Mac bent his head and kissed her. The warm, wet pressure of his lips, the silky slide of her arms around his neck, almost made her forget the last time she'd been carried into a bedroom and the disappointment that had followed. Brian hadn't mentioned frigidity that first night of their marriage, but later, years later, he'd told her he'd known of her "problem" from the beginning.

"Charlotte?"

She opened her eyes, and realized that she had a death grip around his neck and that her mouth hurt from the force she used to press it against his. Abruptly she pulled away, releasing him, and letting her arms free fall to her sides. "I'm sorry. I don't know what—"

"Hey, it's okay." He set her down to stand in front of him and gently brushed a tangled curl off her cheek. "Would you like to talk for a while?" Mac tried to calm the throbbing insistence in his lower body. Even though he'd caught glimpses of her passion before, now she acted more like a virgin than a woman who'd been married. If he didn't know better . . . .

"Talk?" He wanted to talk? Had she scared him with her intensity? She hoped not because the skimming caress of his knuckles over her face was sending currents of heat through her body.

"Sure . . ." Mac's voice faltered when Charlotte turned her head and ran her tongue along one of his fingers. He wondered it she could tell just how far beyond the conversation stage his body was. "We don't have to rush into—"

"I don't want to talk." Charlotte moved against his hardness, threading her hands inside his suit jacket, following the masculine contour of his ribs.

"Me either," Mac moaned as his mouth crushed down against hers. Together they tumbled on to Charlotte's flower-sprinkled bedspread. Lying beside her felt right. He traced the outline of her delicate body. His hands caressed her small, nicely rounded breasts with nipples that, even through the material of her dress and bra, pouted and begged to be suckled; her slightly rounded stomach; and lower to the juncture of her long, sexy legs.

"Oh, my . . ." Charlotte wriggled against his hand as he cupped her intimately. "Oh, my," she breathed, reaching up and pulling his lips down to hers.

Her tongue danced over his, her body arched. Mac pulled up the silky skirt and thrust his hand under the elastic of her panty hose and underwear. Her moist heat drew his fingers to explore the velvety folds and crevices.

The moan she made seemed to come from the depths of her soul. Charlotte's world had narrowed to the two of them, to the marvelous things Mac did to her. Wantonly, she rotated her hips under his palm, conscious of the multifaceted lights that shimmered against her closed eyelids. Her body shivered in anticipation, every nerve cell screaming for release. A roaring began in her head and she bit her bottom lip to contain the sound. His finger moved with excruciating slowness, teasing the swollen nub, taunting her with the promise of more to come.

"Mac." When it came, she couldn't control the

cry of joy that tore through her. Her breasts tingled, her body shook with wave upon shock wave of passion. She grabbed at his shoulders, bunching the charcoal wool of his suit jacket in her clenched fists.

"Mac?" Her body floated back toward earth, landing abruptly when she noticed the lack of his wonderful weight on her.

"Sshh," He soothed leaning over to plant a quick kiss on her cheek. "I'm right here."

Her euphoria returned. It didn't take much imagination to figure out what he was doing. Charlotte heard the coat plop to the floor, the shoes kicked away, the unmistakable sound of a zipper. A smile curved her kiss-reddened lips. Mac certainly could undress quickly. Good. Naked was exactly how she wanted him.

Charlotte forced her eyelids open, amazed at how heavy and lethargic they felt. But there was no way she'd miss seeing Mac. The only light in the room filtered in through the open doorway from the hall. It caressed his broad shoulders and muscular arms. Her gaze moved, past the thick curly mat on his chest, following the narrow strip of brown hair that arrowed lower. She licked suddenly dry lips. Charlotte's imagination had envisioned him before, many times. But in her fantasies, he'd never been this—manly.

A sudden fear clawed its way through the sexual haze that surrounded her. How could someone like him find satisfaction, even contentment with her? Charlotte wanted to crawl under her comforter and bury her head until he realized his mistake and went away.

But he wasn't going to let her. The mattress dipped,

and she felt his long warm body beside her. He propped his head up with his bent arm and stared at her, amusement darkening his eyes. Charlotte was certain he'd seen her ogling him.

"You have too many clothes on, Mrs. Handley." His voice was smooth as silk as he began remedying the situation.

No wonder he could shuffle cards like a pro, Charlotte thought. He had such talented fingers. They could simultaneously undo buttons and fondle the skin they exposed. His head rolled forward on his hand and his hot breath fanned across her flesh moments before his lips grazed her chest.

"Mmmm. You smell good here, too." His nose nuzzled between her breast and Charlotte sucked in her breath as he unhooked the front closure on her bra.

Mac spread open the wispy satin and stared down at her. Even his frequent writer's fantasies about her hadn't conjured up skin this pearly white and smooth. He lathed one rosy tipped nipple and watched in fascination as it tightened, shining wet in the dim light, to a pebbly point. Mac felt fuller and harder than he could ever remember being. He pressed himself against her hip to try and assuage the ache.

"God, Charlotte, you're more beautiful than I'd imagined." His ragged breathing betrayed the burning desire that all but consumed him.

"You thought about what I'd be like?" Surprise tinged her voice.

"Night and day." Mac stripped away her dress and dropped it to the floor.

"Me, too . . . I mean I imagined what you'd be

like. What we'd be like together.'' Charlotte lifted her hips for him to peel away her hose and panties, reveling in his throaty groan.

Mac's eyes swept over her exposed body before he positioned himself above her. ''You fantasized about us?''

Charlotte nodded, wishing he'd lower his body to hers. The space between them seemed charged with zinging electrical current.

''Well, I'll be damned.'' It had never occurred to him that she'd be having the same kind of erotic dreams that had haunted him. He sank down on her softness, using his elbows to protect her from his full weight. She spread open her legs and he had to stop himself from plunging hard and fast into her.

''Mac . . . please, oh, please.'' Charlotte could feel the tip of his hardness throbbing against her. Her hands drifted down his smooth back and clutched his firm buttocks, drawing him closer.

''Charlotte, I don't want to hurt . . . ahhh . . . you.'' He slid slowly into her steamy heat.

''You won't.'' She wrapped her legs around his hips, urging him further, deeper.

This was almost more than he could bear. Again and again he stroked the inside of her body. With each movement she raised her hips, meeting his thrust with one of her own. His hands sank under her and he grasped her buttocks much the same way she held him. Deeper, closer, losing control.

When her trembling began he felt it first deep inside her, then it vibrated along the length of their sweat-slicked bodies. Faster and harder still, he plunged, matching the pulsating rhythm of her shudders with his desperate need. His own climax burst upon him with such powerful force that he buried his face in the cloud of brilliant red hair fanned out against the pillow, sucking in raspy breaths like a man just saved from drowning.

Bright colors exploded inside Charlotte's head. Her hands kneaded his taught muscles, and her chest rose and fell rapidly beneath his. She could feel the pounding of his heart, hear it thundering in matched rhythm with her own. Good Lord, she'd never known anything like this before. The knowledge made her giddy, and before she could stop herself, a small delighted laugh escaped her.

"What's so funny?" Mac's voice murmured huskily in her ear as he rolled to his side, gathering her in his arms as he did.

"Nothing." Her denial lost a lot of credence as laughter bubbled up inside her again.

"Charlotte."

She could tell he wasn't going to let her drop this. "Oh, okay. I was just thinking that now I know."

"Know what?" He propped himself up on an elbow and studied her face, drawing lazy circles on her cheek with his finger.

"What all the fuss is about."

That brought a smile to his lips and Charlotte laughed again. Goodness, she felt wonderful.

"You never knew before?" Mac's finger drifted down the side of her neck.

Charlotte shook her head. "I guess you did?" She shouldn't be asking him that. Of course he knew.

"I probably had a better idea than you, but I have

to admit what just happened is the stuff they write lyrics and prose about.''

"Really?'' Charlotte combed her finger through the springy hair on his chest.

"Really.'' Mac sucked in his breath as her finger grazed his flat nipple.

"Then you don't think I'm frigid?''

"Frigid!'' Mac sat up, looming over her. "For heaven's sake, Charlotte, what ever gave you such a crazy idea?''

Crazy had been to ask him such a stupid question. "Don't laugh at me.'' When would she learn to think before talking?

Mac sobered his expression. He'd thought at first she was joking, but he could tell by her expression—hovering very close to tears—that she wasn't. "I'm not laughing.''

"But you were thinking about it.'' Charlotte raised her hand and touched the indentation in his cheek.

"Well, I'm not now.'' He lay back down beside her, sensing her need to be held. "Are you going to tell me who put such a foolish notion in your head?''

Charlotte buried her face in his chest, loving the musky, masculine smell of him, and said nothing.

Mac tightened his hold. "It was that husband of yours . . . what's his name? . . . Brian. He's the one, isn't he?'' Mac felt her body stiffen.

"I don't want to talk about it.'' Her muffled words tickled his chest.

"Charlotte.''

Goodness sakes, he was a pushy man. But it probably was better to get it out in the open. "Okay! He may have said it a few times . . . maybe more than a few.''

''And you believed him?''

Charlotte pulled away. So what if she had? It was hardly the same as thinking the earth flat or believing in the tooth fairy. She'd had good reason to think her worldly, experienced husband knew what he was talking about. ''What we did . . .'' Her voice faltered as she looked into his understanding eyes. ''It was never like this. I never felt like this.''

''Charlotte, honey.'' He gathered her close, thinking of all the things he'd say to that bastard she'd been married to if he ever ran into him. ''It takes two people to make love. Two people who care and want to please each other.''

''Is that why it was so good just now?''

She was teasing him now. He'd have been able to tell by the laughter in her voice even if he hadn't felt her small hand circle his thigh. ''Mmmm.'' He pulled her closer, telling her all she needed to know about his renewed need to please and be pleased.

_____ **NINE** _____

He liked to cuddle.

Charlotte smiled and snuggled closer to Mac's nude body. She'd awakened only moments ago with the strangest feeling that something wonderful had happened. It had taken only the weight of Mac's leg across hers, his hand cupping her breast, the sound of his even breathing, to bring all of last night spinning to the forefront of her mind.

Something wonderful *had* happened. She'd discovered what it was like to really love a man. And if he didn't feel the same toward her, well, at least he cared for her. By his own definition of making love, he'd proved that to her on more than one occasion last night.

And now to find out that he liked to cuddle while he slept—it was like frosting on the cake. This closeness to another human being had been one of the things she'd missed in her marriage. One of the many things, she thought, remembering her other discovery from last night. How could she ever have believed she knew anything about sex? She tried to remember what she had told Elizabeth during their mother-daughter talk about reproduction, and decided a refresher course was probably in order.

Mac shifted in his sleep, placing his hair-roughened chest more firmly against her back, and a current of desire raced through Charlotte. She'd better get out of bed, away from his body, before she pounced on him and woke him up. The poor man had earned the right to sleep in.

Carefully, trying not to disturb him, Charlotte inched herself toward the edge of the bed.

"Where're you going?" A sleep-rusty voice ruffled the hair around her ear.

"I thought I'd get up," she whispered. He didn't sound fully awake.

"Can't." His hand tightened on her breast.

"Why not?" He was obviously a man of few words in the morning, but she wasn't sure about actions. Did he realize what his thumb was doing to her nipple?

"Haven't had my 'good-morning kiss' yet."

He knew. Charlotte could tell the moment he rolled her over on her back. His whiskered smile was lazy, but his keen eyes zeroed in on her distended nipple before focusing on her face.

His kiss was deep and thorough and before he'd finished, he lay more on top of Charlotte than on the bed.

"Feels to me as if you have more than a kiss in mind here." Charlotte moved her body against his erection.

"You're right. But this early in the morning I couldn't think of a way to say it that didn't sound crude." His hand left her breast to tangle in the triangle of curly hair between her legs. "I figured I'd just kind of slide into it." The movement of his fingers mirrored his words.

"Mmmm." There was no way Charlotte could pretend this wasn't exactly what she'd wanted. Her body arched toward his, opening like the petals of a sun-kissed flower.

"You're not sore are you?" Mac raised his head. He'd made love to her last night more times than he'd thought humanly possible. When he awoke to find her in his arms, he'd wanted her all over again. But he felt certain her body wasn't use to this much action.

Sore! He wasn't going to stop. Was he? Charlotte threaded her fingers through his sleep-shaggy hair, smiling at the spark of desire that brightened his beautiful eyes. "No, I'm not sore," she whispered, tugging his head lower.

"You're certain?" his tone teased. "Not here?" He brushed his lips across hers.

"No." Charlotte breathed.

"Or here?" His whiskered chin grazed across her breast before his tongue wet the straining tip.

Charlotte shook her head, beyond speech. She ached, she throbbed. He was driving her crazy.

"What about here?" he said, his husky voice fanning the curls at the juncture of her thighs.

Charlotte caught her breath on a gasp and held it. Her heart pounded in her chest; and when he touched her with his mouth, a buzzing like the swarming of a million bees began in her head. Without thinking she grasped handfuls of sheet, twisting and pulling them away from the mattress.

His tongue was scalding hot and moving, always moving. It rubbed against the heat of her, while his hands held her bottom. She squirmed and writhed, thrashing her head back and forth on the pillow. When the tremors started, Charlotte thought she'd burst into flames. Every cell of her body tingled and strained toward him.

Mac raised his head, looking up over her smooth white stomach. Her breasts were tighter than he'd ever seen them, and her body still quivered with the aftershock of her release. He combed his fingers through the red curls still damp from his kisses and his manhood ached. "God, Charlotte. You look like you're on fire for me." He inched his way up her body, covering her with his heat.

"I am . . . oh, Mac . . . I am." Her breathless voice caught on a gasp as he thrust inside, filling her completely.

Charlotte stood under the shower, letting the warm water ooze down her body. She'd read somewhere that some people especially enjoyed showers because the splashing water droplets released ozones or electrons or something like that. The explanation had been more complex than she'd wanted to understand, but she'd decided then that she was one of those people who could pick up the Ping-Ponging atomic particles.

"Mmmm." Charlotte stuck her head under the rushing water, soaking her hair. She'd left Mac in bed, sleeping. When he'd rolled off her, flopping onto his back with a self-satisfied groan, she'd wriggled out of bed. Sleep was way beyond her grasp now. She felt more like climbing Mt. Everest or flying solo around the world—maybe even without a plane.

Humming, she squirted a dollop of rose-scented shampoo into her hand and worked it into her hair. The foamy lather squished through her fingers and slithered erotically down her shoulders, between her breasts. Lovely memories of last night and this morning filled her mind like the fragrant steam filled the shower stall. The sudden drop in water pressure caught Charlotte off guard.

She stopped singing and cocked her ear out of the stream of water. Someone was in the bathroom with her. "Mac?" She peeked around the shower curtain, relieved, though surprised, to see him standing in front of the sink. She'd had a momentary vision of Norman Bates slashing his way through the plastic curtain. Going to that movie had been a mistake.

Mac stopped trying to make a thick lather on his face with a bar of soap, and caught Charlotte's eye in the bathroom mirror. "You need some shaving cream, lady."

"I'll put it on my shopping list," she assured. After getting over the initial shock of finding him in her bathroom, Charlotte decided she liked it. This was another little intimacy she wasn't used to sharing with a man.

She watched as he picked up a pink, disposable razor and looked at it questioningly. "Does this thing work?"

Charlotte suppressed a laugh. "I use it."

He turned to face her, and the gleam in his eye was down right wicked. "I don't recall your legs being hairy, so I guess it does." His gaze was a vivid reminder that he had first hand knowledge of her legs and every other part of her anatomy.

Charlotte swallowed and stuck her head under the shower spray. He was doing it to her again. Her knees felt like melting butter. With very little effort she could imagine herself slipping down the drain. How could he be so sexy dressed like that? Charlotte visualized what he'd looked like, leaning against the sink—the lower half of his face covered with a thin layer of gray bubbles, and a pink flowered towel wrapped around his narrow waist. Though she tried not to, Charlotte began to laugh.

"What?" Mac called.

"Oh, nothing." She didn't sound convincing. Especially since her laughter now sounded more like giggling.

The shower curtain shot open!

Charlotte gasped, trying to think of a way to cover herself. By the expression on his face as his gaze drifted over her, the transparent water wasn't doing the trick. The cooler bathroom air chilled her skin, hardened her nipples.

"Laughing at me were you, Miss Charlotte?"

Charlotte bit her bottom lip and shook her head, sending droplets of water spinning through the air. He'd shaved off the soap, but he still wore the towel. It struck her that he resembled pictures she'd seen of Greek gods. They were usually broad shouldered, manly, and dressed in a skimpy scrap of material, but she didn't think their scraps were pink or, worse yet, flowered. Fresh laughter bubbled up.

At his questioning expression, all she could do was point to the towel.

He glanced down at himself and his bark of laughter showed Charlotte he shared her amusement. "Can I help it if everything in this house is covered with blossoms?"

"I like flowers."

"So do I, but on towels?" He gave the one he wore a casual flick and it dropped to the floor. Nude as the day he was born, he stepped into the shower and closed the curtain behind him.

The stall wasn't large, and Charlotte faded back against the cold tile to give him room. There was certainly nothing about him she could laugh at now. She'd never shared a shower before, except in her fantasies, and she groped for something to say to make her appear less of a novice. "What color are your towels?" Couldn't she come up with something better than that?

He stopped rubbing the bar of soap over his hairy chest. "White, I think." He paused. "Maybe blue. Yeah, some white, some blue."

"I see."

Mac shrugged. She probably thought him a real boob for not knowing the color of his linens, but the truth was, his housekeeper bought them, washed them, and put them away. All he did was dry off—and his mind was usually occupied with something other than the task at hand. Lately it had been thinking about the redheaded woman standing in the shower.

"Want me to wash your back?" He grinned; and

before Charlotte could answer, he'd wrapped his arms around her and was working up a lather. "You have a nice spine." A finger drew an imaginary line down the center of her back. "Straight," he added.

"My mother believed in good posture." Charlotte closed her eyes and let her body enjoy the sensations he evoked.

"Smart woman." Mac turned her so the spray could rinse her back. Then he quickly finished washing himself.

"How about a kiss before I leave you to your shower?" He loomed over her, his hair slicked back with water, his eyelashes spiky and tipped with shimmering diamond droplets.

Charlotte threaded her arms around his waist. "A kiss is all you said you wanted this morning."

"Yeah, well, a kiss is all you're getting right now, you brazen hussy." He licked a drop of water off the tip of her nose, "I'm not superman, you know?"

Charlotte managed to refrain from saying you couldn't prove it by her, as his lips met hers. The kiss was warm and wet, and with their naked, slick bodies touching in so many interesting places, more than a little wild.

When Mac pulled away, his breathing was uneven. "Give me an hour or two," he teased. "And I'll be able to do better."

"You . . ." Charlotte slapped at his taut rear as he jumped, laughing from the stall.

"Better come on out of there, Charlotte, or you'll turn into a prune."

"I'm not finished. Someone interrupted me." Charlotte stuck her head out of the curtain. She watched him towel-dry his hair.

"I was afraid you'd use all the hot water." He turned and winked at her. "Hurry up and I'll fix you some breakfast. What do you want?"

"I could eat a horse." Charlotte scrubbed at her stomach and legs. She thought she heard him mumble something about all her recent activities making her hungry, but when she stuck her head back out and asked, he laughingly denied it.

"I don't know how to prepare horse, but I'll look around your kitchen and see what I can find—after my sports fix."

"Your what?" She'd never finish her shower at this rate, and the water was starting to cool.

He wrapped the towel around his hips. "You do get the morning paper, don't you?"

"Sure. It's probably out on the front porch." Charlotte turned off the faucet.

"Good. I have to see what happened in the world of sports while I . . . slept." He bobbed his brows and gave her one last leering look before leaving the room.

Mac stuck his bare feet on the coffee table and opened the paper to the sports page. Before opening the front door, he'd only pulled on his suit pants. He sat, shirtless, on the couch. He'd been in too much of a hurry last night to worry about hanging up clothes, and it showed. Before they went anyplace today, he and Charlotte were going to have to stop by his house, so he could change. He glanced down at the headlines. "Hey, the Redskins are playing at home tomorrow. You want to go?"

"To the football game?" Charlotte yelled back to

the living room from her bedroom as she knotted her terry cloth robe around her waist. "How would we get in?" She remembered Brian being on some waiting list for tickets that was hundreds of years long.

"My uncle has season tickets that he almost never uses."

"Oh." She tried running the comb through her hair. Damn, she'd forgotten the conditioner. "I don't know if I should leave Elizabeth alone all day tomorrow."

"She can come, too."

"Your uncle can get three tickets? Is he connected with the Mafia or something?" Charlotte heard his laughter drift down the hall.

"I don't know. You can ask him tomorrow." Mac wondered how his distinguished uncle, Senator Dodson, would react to such a question. The old guy was a pretty liberal thinker; he'd probably get a hoot out of it. He'd like Charlotte, of that Mac was certain. Mac had mentioned her more than once when he'd visited his uncle's Georgetown home over Thanksgiving. He hadn't told his only living relative that Charlotte was the reason he'd decided to accept his invitation. Mac hadn't explained that after being around Charlotte and her daughter, he couldn't bare the thought of spending the holiday alone.

Mac closed the paper and let it drop to the floor. Now what he really needed to do was explain some things to Charlotte. He rubbed the back of his neck. She probably wasn't going to like this, especially since he hadn't told her sooner.

"Charlotte? Could you come out here a minute?"

"My hair's still wet."

"Wrap something around it. I need to talk to you." All of a sudden it seemed urgent that she know—about his wealth, about Vietnam. He needed her to understand.

If he hadn't been so concerned about Charlotte's reaction, he might have heard the front door open. But even if he had, everything happened so quickly there was nothing he could do. One second he sat alone in the living room waiting for Charlotte; the next, Elizabeth was there, staring down at him. All he could do was stare back.

"What's so important you can't wait till I'm dry?" Charlotte came padding into the room, feet bare, head wrapped "Aunt Jamima style" in a towel.

She stopped, and Mac's mind freeze-framed the look of horror on her face when she saw her daughter.

"I forgot my riding boots. They're in my closet. I'll just get them," Elizabeth mumbled, keeping her gaze carefully lowered.

Mac wasn't surprised that Elizabeth recovered first. After all, she didn't have anything to feel guilty about. And damnit there was no way his being here could look like anything other than what it was. He might as well have big red letters across his bare chest stating, "I spent the night with your mother."

"Lizzy." Charlotte started down the hall after her daughter. "Let me explain." But Elizabeth was already coming toward her, riding boots in hand.

"I better go."

"Elizabeth!" Charlotte was beginning to sound frantic.

"Ali's grandfather is waiting in the car." Elizabeth backed toward the door. "I'm really sorry. Bye, Mom, Mr. McQuade."

The latch clicked in place, and Mac could hear Elizabeth's footsteps racing down the porch steps. He took a deep breath and looked toward Charlotte. She'd sunk onto the couch and buried her face in her hands. He couldn't tell if she was crying.

He slid across the pillow, touching the gentle curve of her neck. "Charlotte?"

"Don't!" Charlotte jerked away as if he'd burned her. She brushed away a tear and stared straight ahead. "I think you better leave."

"Oh, hell, Charlotte, why?" Mac was immediately sorry for his profanity, but she was frustrating him beyond belief.

"Why! You have the nerve to ask me that? My daughter just walked in here and saw you . . . like that . . . and me . . ." Words seemed to fail her.

"You think I don't know that. I was here remember." Mac stood and followed her to the window.

"Then there's no need for explanations—just leave."

Mac ignored her request. "Listen, I know this whole thing is embarrassing—hey, *I* was embarrassed. But Elizabeth's a reasonable kid. I'm sure when we explain it to her—"

"You're not explaining anything. She's my daughter."

"Fine." Mac felt his temper cracking and tried to hold it together. Why was she making such a federal case out of this? "You want to do the talking, that's okay by me. I'll just be here to offer moral support."

"Ha!" Charlotte let go of the curtain she'd been clutching and stomped into the kitchen. Mac followed.

"What's that suppose to mean?"

Charlotte slammed the refrigerator shut when he

started to reach for the orange juice. Why didn't he just leave?

"Well?"

"It means you're a fine one to be talking about moral support. Immoral, maybe. Oh, why didn't I listen to my own common sense? I knew better than to get involved with you."

Mac was glad she didn't hear the expletive he said under his breath. This was getting them nowhere. Perhaps he should leave and let her settle down. "Listen." He tried to sound calm. "I'll get dressed and go. Talk to Elizabeth, and I'll call you later. Maybe we can all go someplace for dinner."

"No!"

"Okay. I'll stop over and we can—"

"No," Charlotte repeated. "Don't come over, don't call. Ever."

He said the curse word again, but this time she heard him. And this time he didn't care. "What are you talking about?" He grabbed her shoulders, forcing her to look at him. "You mean to tell me you're going to let this . . . this misunderstanding come between us . . . come between what we had last night?" Now he was beginning to sound panicked.

Charlotte sucked in her breath on a sob. Oh, God, what was she giving up? She bit her bottom lip to keep fresh tears from flowing down her face. She wanted to tell him about the other time, the day she and Elizabeth had come home early from her mother's and found Brian and his latest paramour in bed. What was the use? Mac would just try to tell her it wasn't the same. Well, maybe it wasn't, but she couldn't handle this. "Mother's taken a lover" was not the explanation she wanted to give her daughter.

Mac stared down into her face, willing her to say something. She didn't. He loosened his grip and let his hands slide down her terry cloth clad arms. "All right. Have it your way." His hands dropped to his sides as if he were wearing wrist weights. "But I think you're making a big mistake." *Just leave now, Mac, before you say something you'll regret.*

Oh, hell, he was tired of being noble; and besides, what else could she do? Break off their relationship? "I'll tell you something else, Charlotte. You don't have to worry that I'll call, or drop over. In fact, you don't have to worry about my corrupting influence any more. You won't see me until you decide to grow up and face the truth."

Mac took a deep breath and forced himself to look into her pain-filled, blue eyes. "Your mother's the kind of person who, given half the chance, would run anybody's life. And I think you gave her the chance. Then there's your ex-husband. He sounds like a real manipulator, too. Now you're trying to give the task over to a sweet kid like Elizabeth. And you know what?" He didn't wait for her to answer. "I don't think she wants the job."

Boy, he'd really blown it now. Mac stood in Charlotte's bedroom and yanked on a sock. She'd never speak to him again after that parting shot. *Kick them when their down, McQuade,* that ought to be his motto. Not that he didn't believe a lot of what he'd said, but she hadn't deserved the way he'd said it. Besides, she was trying to pull her life together. That was one of the things he loved about her.

Mac stopped jamming his shirttail into his pants as

the last thought crystallized in his mind. There was no doubt about it now. He loved her. He loved Charlotte Handley—and she never wanted to see him again.

Well, he'd see about that. Mac stuffed his tie in his coat pocket and headed for the door. He'd give her time to calm down, and to talk to Elizabeth. Then, regardless of what he'd said, he'd be back. Damned if he wouldn't.

Charlotte paced off the distance between the front door and the kitchen—for at least the twentieth time. It was after four o'clock, so where was Elizabeth? Charlotte interrupted her routine to flop down on the couch. She ran her fingers through her curly hair and sighed. This had been the longest, most miserable day of her life.

It had started out so promising. Mac. How could she have kicked him out like that? Charlotte jumped to her feet. There she was again, thinking of Mac when it was Elizabeth whom she should be worried about. Elizabeth whom she owed her allegiance.

Mac should never have said those things to her, even if some of them were true. Her mother had dominated her for eighteen years, but she didn't anymore. And Brian. Well, he had taken right up where Ida had left off. But Elizabeth, she wasn't the same at all. As Mac had said, she was just a nice kid. All Charlotte wanted to do was be a good mother, and good mother's did not parade their half-dressed lovers around in front of their daughters.

"Mom!"

Charlotte grabbed the edge of the sink. She hadn't heard Elizabeth come in. "I'm in the kitchen, Lizzy."

"Hi." Elizabeth dropped her bulging duffle bag right inside the kitchen doorway and slid onto a chair. "Boy, am I tired."

Charlotte opened the oven and checked on the homemade pizza. Fixing that had taken up some of her long afternoon. "Did you enjoy your riding lesson?"

"Yeah, but I'd forgotten how sore your leg muscles could get. We did some jumps today, and I got to ride Jo-jo."

"That's great, honey." Charlotte made a mental note to call Allison's grandfather and thank him. Driving the girls all the way to the stables west of Richmond where Elizabeth used to ride was beyond the call of duty.

Elizabeth stood up, brushing dust from her gray riding pants. "I guess I better go get cleaned up. What's for dinner?"

"Pizza. And it's almost ready." Why were they making small talk when there was so much that needed to be said?

"I'll hurry." Elizabeth grabbed her overnight bag. "Oh, is Mr. McQuade having dinner with us?"

"No!" Charlotte realized she'd spoken too loudly in the small room. "No, he's not, Lizzy."

"Too bad," Elizabeth said before swinging the duffle bag over her shoulder and leaving the kitchen.

"Now, just what was that suppose to mean?" Charlotte mumbled to herself. By all rights Elizabeth shouldn't want to see Mac again. Charlotte had spent the day worrying about what was going to happen Monday morning when they had to face each other in school.

The smell of burning dough jerked Charlotte's thoughts back to the here and now. The pizza! She grabbed a hot pad and pulled the round pan from the oven. Gingerly, she lifted the pie and examined the underside. Not too bad. She'd burned things worse in her time.

"Lizzy, dinner's ready!" And then some, Charlotte thought, scraping off the worst of the charred dough.

"Coming, Mom."

Charlotte waited until they were both seated at the table with a generous slice of thick-crusted pizza. "Elizabeth, I need to talk to you."

"Sure, Mom."

"About this morning."

"Gee, I'm really sorry about that. I should have—"

"Lizzy!" It had taken Charlotte a moment to realize her daughter was apologizing. "I don't mean what you did. I'm talking about me . . . and Mr. McQuade."

"Oh." Elizabeth took another bite of pizza.

Charlotte stared at her daughter. She'd certainly expected more of a reaction. Two years ago when Elizabeth had helped her mother carry some packages into her bedroom, and they'd walked in on her father and some woman named Lisa in bed, she hadn't acted like this.

Charlotte tried again. "He shouldn't have been here. And . . . well, you don't have to worry about something like that happening again."

"You're getting married?" Elizabeth's blue eyes lit up like Christmas trees.

"No." Charlotte shook her head. "No, Lizzy. What ever gave you that idea?"

"Well, you said . . . I don't know. I just thought maybe you were."

"That's not what I meant." Charlotte refilled her daughter's milk glass. "Mr. McQuade and I aren't going to see each other any more." As much as she'd rehearsed this all afternoon, it still hurt to say it.

"Why?"

"Because . . ." What were her reasons? "Because of this morning. I know how you must have felt when you walked in and saw Mac . . . Mr. McQuade here."

"Embarrassed!" Elizabeth took another bite of pizza. "But I think Mr. McQuade was more upset than me. And you, Mom. You should have seen your face."

Laughing. Her daughter was laughing. Was she hysterical?

"Elizabeth."

"What?" Apparently her mother's tone sobered her, because she stopped giggling.

"I had a right to look—how ever I looked. You'd walked in on . . . It was like before . . . Oh, Lizzy, I just don't want you to think I'm like your father."

"Hey, Mom." Elizabeth came around the table and hugged her mother. "I'd never think that. I knew about Dad a long time before . . . well, you know."

Charlotte wrapped her arms around Elizabeth's waist. "You did?"

"Sure. Our neighbor, Mrs. Adams, was telling someone about him on the telephone one time when I was visiting Cary. She didn't see me in the hall, and when I heard who she was talking about . . . I listened. I got the feeling a lot of people knew. But I just didn't want you to find out.''

"Oh, Lizzy. I'm sorry you had to learn about it that way.''

Elizabeth shrugged and went back to her seat. "Dad shouldn't have been doing that stuff when he was married to you, but you and Mr. McQuade aren't married to anybody else.''

Charlotte marveled at the fourteen-year-old mind. Elizabeth seemed to have everything settled to her own satisfaction. However, she'd forgotten one thing. "We aren't married to each other, either.''

Elizabeth stopped chewing and took a swig of milk. "But that's what I mean. You should be.''

TEN

Lost.

She might as well admit it. She was lost. Charlotte peered through the windshield, willing a gas station . . . anything to appear. But nothing did. Ahead of her she saw nothing but more twisted road lined with bare skeletons of equally twisted trees.

The area was probably very pleasant when it wasn't shrouded by a cloak of darkness, Charlotte conceded, wishing she'd had the forethought—and patience to wait until tomorrow before rushing off in search of Mac.

"Oh, no," she mumbled to herself. "You couldn't wait till the light of day to tell him." She'd had to do it right away. The echo of Elizabeth's words declaring that her mother and Mr. McQuade should be married hadn't even died away when Charlotte had jumped to her feet. Everything had seemed very clear at that moment.

She and Mac should be married! She knew it. Elizabeth knew it. Now all that remained was to convince Mac. With that thought paramount in her mind, she'd dashed to her car and driven off into the darkness. Charlotte shook her head, loosening the scarf she'd thrown around it.

"Don't be so melodramatic," Charlotte warned herself in a muffled whisper. She hadn't run off willy-nilly. Hadn't she called Allison's mother, a woman she already owed a favor, to ask her for another?

At least Elizabeth was safe, even though she was surprised to be spending another night at her friend's house. Charlotte slid her elbow back along the inside of the car door. The plunger was still down. Good. The door hadn't miraculously unlocked itself.

Get a grip on yourself. She wasn't afraid of the dark. She wasn't. But there was something about this night. The way the wind bid the ominous black clouds to play hide-and-seek with the silvery moon sent chills dancing up Charlotte's spine, even as the car heater blew puffs of hot air in her face. It was the kind of night that made you believe in werewolves— straight from a Gothic novel.

"Oh, for heaven's sake." The thready glow of the Volvo's headlights veered to the left as Charlotte followed the road. That's when she saw it. At first, Charlotte thought it might be a trick of the moon, but as she drove on, she knew it wasn't.

Lights. There were lights shimmering and twinkling through the stark, swaying branches of a thick stand of trees. Charlotte turned into a winding driveway that seemed to go on forever. When she finally reached the end, she stopped the car and stared.

The lights came from a house, a large, rambling house. Though she could make out very little in the darkness, it appeared to be made of wood, and it blended very well with its rustic surroundings. If there was a lawn, Charlotte couldn't see it. It seemed as if the natural environment had been allowed to grow and flourish almost to the front door.

Charlotte's hands tightened on the steering wheel. She was going to have to get out of the car and go to that front door. Alone. "Oh, don't be such a wimp." Charlotte shoved open the car door before she could change her mind.

The house probably belonged to a nice, elderly couple who raised cats, not werewolves. A nice, *rich* elderly couple, Charlotte amended as she crunched up the crushed shell walkway. All she had to do was tell them she was lost, and ask directions back to the main road. While the husband drew her a map, his wife would no doubt insist on making her a cup of tea. Then she'd go home and call Mac.

Charlotte took a deep breath and knocked on the door. Women of the nineties did this all the time, she told herself. Of course, women of the nineties took self-defense classes and carried mace. Charlotte wondered if she could use her hairbrush as a weapon in an emergency.

The door opened, bathing Charlotte in a puddle of soft light that carried with it the mellow strains of a rhythm and blues melody. She kept her eyes carefully lowered. The elderly man wasn't wearing any shoes. The thought hit Charlotte that for an old man he had awfully sexy feet.

She swallowed. "I'm sorry to bother you, but you see, I'm lost, and if you could just tell me how—"

"Charlotte?"

Her eyes shot up. "Mac?" Charlotte threw herself against him, burying her face in the worn cotton of his sweatshirt. "Oh, Mac."

Mac wrapped his arms around Charlotte, trying to stop her shivering. "Honey, are you all right?" His words were muffled against her hair.

"I'm okay." Charlotte pushed away from Mac, feeling utterly foolish. "I just thought I was lost . . . oh, I guess I said that." She made a nervous gesture with her hand, conscious that his arms were still around her. "Anyway, I thought I was lost and stopped here for directions. You don't have many neighbors, do you?"

"None close." Mac reached behind her and closed the door. "Come in and sit down." Mac took Charlotte's coat and led her around to the couch. "Would you like a drink?"

"Well." Charlotte glanced down at the end table and noticed three empty beer bottles. Obviously, *he'd* had something to drink. "All right."

He looked at her expectantly. "What would you like?"

"Uh . . ." She glanced again at the bottles. "Beer will be fine."

"I have soft drinks."

"I know how to drink beer," Charlotte said defensively. It wasn't bad enough that she'd gotten lost, then practically thrown herself into his arms. Now he acted like he planned to card her. Maybe coming here hadn't been such a good idea.

When Mac left the room, Charlotte took the opportunity to look around. She could probably fit her entire house into this one room. And books! She'd never seen this many anyplace that didn't have the word library printed over the front door.

"Here you are."

Charlotte glanced up guiltily. She'd been so busy ogling her surroundings, she hadn't noticed him come back into the room. He placed a glass, presumably for her, on the low, natural pine table in front of the couch. Two bottles swung from the fingers of his other hand. He twisted the caps off and poured one into her glass; taking a healthy swig from the other. Charlotte watched the strong muscles of his throat as he swallowed. She took a sip of her own drink. Suddenly, she was very thirsty.

Bitter. Charlotte tried not to grimace as the vile brew burned down her throat. How could she have forgotten how much she disliked the taste of beer? Apparently, Mac didn't share her opinion because he took another gulp from his bottle before sitting on the couch beside her and settling it between his legs.

"You talked to Elizabeth?" Mac's question was abrupt and clipped. Now that he knew Charlotte was okay, he wondered how in the hell he was suppose to explain this house. More importantly, how was he to justify the fact that he hadn't told her before? Why did opening one door of his past make him fear that all the others would follow?

"Yes." Charlotte impulsively emptied her glass. He sounded so angry.

"And?"

"You were right. She wasn't nearly as traumatized as I'd thought she'd be." He just stared at her, his blue-green eyes unwavering. Why didn't he take her in his arms again?

Mac took another swig of beer. He'd spent a long, miserable day trying to convince himself that he was better off without Charlotte. He'd been happy before he met her; at least he hadn't been unhappy. Maybe, just maybe, he'd tried to convince himself, he'd been wrong about being in love with her. But, now, seeing her sitting in front of him, he knew the truth.

"Mac." Charlotte tried to ignore his silence. She'd come this far. She had to tell him. "I should have told you this morning why I was so worried. You see, this isn't the first time Elizabeth has had this kind of experience. Oh, she never walked in on me before." Charlotte smiled at the relieved expression on Mac's face. "She walked in on her father." Charlotte's smile faded.

"Elizabeth and I were together. We opened the bedroom door . . . and there he was . . . with another woman."

Mac moved closer.

"So you see, I thought, well, I didn't want her to think . . ."

"That you were like her father."

Charlotte nodded and Mac gave into temptation and pulled her close. "She wouldn't think that."

Charlotte smiled into the soft cotton sweatshirt. "Elizabeth told me as much this afternoon." Charlotte could hear Mac's heart beating in her ear. When she'd told him to leave this morning, she must have forgotten how comforting that sound could be.

"It must have been tough on you."

"Oh, no, she really was very reasonable." Charlotte lifted her head to look up at him.

Mac threaded his fingers through the red curls and

gently drew her back against his chest. He loved the feel of her there. "I mean the other time . . . with Brian."

"Mmmm," Charlotte agreed. "It certainly wasn't pleasant. But I'd known about his affairs for a long time. At least I'd suspected that he had them."

"And you stayed with him?"

"I know it must seem strange to you—that a wife could doubt her husband's fidelity and do nothing. But I didn't know for sure, and I thought Elizabeth would be better off if we stayed together. And I guess I was scared. I hadn't finished college, had no marketable skill."

"But you left." There was pride in his voice.

"When I opened that door and saw them—I knew what I had to do—what I should have done long before then." She nestled closer against Mac. His large hands stroked her back.

Mac leaned against the pillows, wrapping her more tightly in his arms. A burning log in the fireplace shifted, falling against the grate in a shower of sparks. Mac glanced at the expanse of window overlooking the river, and remembered the fantasy he'd had of them nestled here together.

"I didn't love him." Charlotte's voice, hardly more than a whisper, was muffled against Mac's neck. The sensual motion of his hands stopped. "I used to feel guilty about it. I even wondered if I could ever love any man . . . until . . . ."

Mac's fingers circled her neck, angling her chin up. "Till what?"

The question was magnified by his eyes, intense, deep as an ocean. Charlotte arched forward, her lips just grazing his. "Until now."

The crush of his mouth took her breath away. It was hot and wet, tasting faintly of beer. And oh, how wonderful it felt. Charlotte burrowed her hands beneath his sweatshirt, running them along the muscles of his stomach. She could feel his hard weight pushing her back into the soft pillows of the couch.

"Charlotte?" They were both gasping for breath when their lips separated.

"What?" His teeth nibbled at her ear lobe and his talented fingers had already reached under her sweater to unfasten her bra.

"Elizabeth isn't in your car is she?"

"No . . . hmm . . . why?" She wriggled her body until her breast fit snugly in his palm.

"I just don't think this would be a good time for her to walk in." With one swift motion, he pulled the sweater over her head and tossed it on the floor. His sweatshirt followed.

Charlotte closed her eyes as his mat of golden brown hair brushed across her chest. "There's no one else here, is there?" Certainly he had to share the mortgage payment for this place with at least ten roommates.

"No." His aggressive mouth followed the curve of her jaw. "The housekeeper doesn't work on weekends."

Housekeeper? Had he said housekeeper? Charlotte's mind had passed the point of rational functioning, so she wasn't sure. Maybe she should ask him. He unsnapped her pants. Maybe not.

"God, you're beautiful, Charlotte." His voice vibrated through her as he followed the path of her descending jeans. "All creamy white and rosy red."

"Mmmm." The man should write books, books of poetry.

Mac knelt by the couch and untied Charlotte's tennis shoes. He tugged them off, then removed her socks. Now he could pull the jeans off her long, graceful legs. She was lying radiantly naked before him. He reached out a finger and ran it lazily along the arch of her foot. She jerked away.

"What's wrong?" His tongue wet a splattering of freckles on her knee.

"Ticklish." Was that her voice? She hardly recognized the low, breathy tones.

"Where . . . here?" He touched her again and she instinctively pulled her feet away, folding her legs at the knees.

"Hmm . . ." Mac's grin was wicked as he unzipped his jeans, pulling them and a pair of white briefs off. "I'll have to remember that." With graceful ease he settled down between her raised thighs. "Am I too heavy?"

"No. You feel good."

Mac eased into her fire.

"Oh, yeah . . . good," he agreed on a raspy breath.

Charlotte locked her fingers on the sides of Mac's head. Her gaze held his and for a moment they shared the wondrous sensations of their coupling. "Love me, Mac," she whispered, arching her body toward his. "Love me. . . ."

Mac moved slowly, almost withdrawing before gently sliding back to fill her completely. Once, twice, he repeated the sensual motion. "I do, Charlotte. I do."

His movement quickened. Faster and faster he plunged. She met each thrust. Her hips rotating. Meeting him. Drawing him further into her heat. Her scalding, searing heat.

Charlotte bit her lip to trap the scream of pleasure that swelled up inside her, but the sound escaped anyway. Or was it Mac groaning against her ear that she heard? Charlotte grabbed his shoulders, digging her fingers into his muscles as the spasms passed through her. There were the lights again, exploding, shattering into all the colors of the universe.

"Oh, Charlotte." Mac collapsed on top of her. "I'm exhausted." He rolled over, reaching across the back of the couch and dragging an afghan over them. In less than a minute his even breathing announced that he'd fallen asleep.

Charlotte sighed. "Mac?" There were things she needed to ask him, but it appeared she'd get no answers from him now. And she was tired. Neither of them had slept much last night, and today had been draining. Besides, as unused to drinking as she was, the beer was having a drugging effect on her. She snuggled up against Mac's side on the wide corduroy sofa and closed her eyes.

Faint whispers of dawn filtered through the window when she opened them again. Mac's face was turned toward her and she brushed her lips across his, smiling when he twitched his mouth in his sleep. Charlotte slipped out from under the crocheted blanket. The room was cold, and she grabbed Mac's sweatshirt, pulling it over her head. The hem hit her mid-thigh. Wrapping her arms around herself, she went in search of a bathroom.

Charlotte padded off in the direction Mac had taken last night. Her bare feet skimmed across the wide pine planks that led from the huge Oriental rug surrounding the sofa to the rough brick flooring in the kitchen. What a kitchen! It was huge, containing every conceivable appliance. She ran her fingers along the gleaming, stainless tiles.

"I always find this room too stark, but Miss Gracie likes it."

Charlotte turned at the sound of Mac's voice. His hair was a tumble of sleep-tossed shaggy curls. He'd pulled on his jeans but hadn't snapped them. "Miss Gracie?"

"My housekeeper." He walked over to the center island and leaned his hip against it, staring at her. "Do you think some flowered wallpaper would make it any homier?"

So he *had* mentioned a housekeeper last night. How could a school teacher afford this house and a housekeeper? Charlotte remembered his question and glanced around at the white walls. "Possibly. Uh, I was looking for a bathroom."

"Through there." He motioned to a closed door off the kitchen. "Or if you want to get cleaned up, you can use mine."

"No . . . no. That's okay." Charlotte hurried off in the direction he'd indicated. She needed to be alone for a moment to think.

When she'd closed the door behind her, Charlotte turned on the fancy faucets and splashed water on her face. Something just wasn't right here.

She'd teased him about his family being involved with the Mafia and now she wondered if that could be a possibility. She'd seen this movie once. . . . ."Oh, stop it," she admonished the dripping face in the mirror. "Mac wouldn't do anything like that."

Charlotte reached for a towel—a white one—and dried herself. How could she be certain what Mac would do? She'd thought she knew him. But now . . . Charlotte tried to remember everything he'd told her about himself. It certainly wasn't a long list. He'd been born on Long Island, been married, divorced, fought in Vietnam, and had an uncle who could get his hands on three Redskins tickets.

Not a whole lot to know about the person you loved—the person you wanted to marry and live with for the rest of your life.

Charlotte stayed in the bathroom as long as she could, thinking, trying to figure Mac out. When she finally opened the door, he stood in the kitchen pouring water into an automatic coffee maker. He turned and smiled, tentatively. It didn't take a genius to see that he'd been thinking, too.

"Want some coffee? It'll be ready in a minute." He stuck the glass pot into the machine and turned it on.

Charlotte shook her head. "No, none for me, thanks."

"Another beer?"

Charlotte smiled. "No, I think I've had my limit—for the year." He could make her want to laugh even when she didn't feel happy. Was that as important as knowing about your lover's past?

Those blue-green eyes that had captivated her from the moment she'd seen them, assessed her slowly from head to bare toes.

"You look good in that." He pointed to the sweatshirt Charlotte had forgotten she wore.

She just stood in the middle of the kitchen and said nothing.

"I guess you're not in the mood for compliments this morning, huh?"

"Mac, I—"

"You want to know about this." He swung his arm around in an impatient gesture. The time for explanations was long past.

"I want to know about you."

"Okay," he said defensively. "You may have guessed by my surroundings that I'm rich. Very rich. Don't even ask how much money I have because, frankly, I don't know. I pay accountants to keep track of that." His eyes skewered hers. "And you don't like rich people, right?"

"Is that why you didn't tell me? Because you thought I wouldn't like you?" She tried to understand.

"No!" Mac strode out of the kitchen and plopped down on the sofa. He may have tried to tell himself that was the reason, but he knew it wasn't.

Charlotte followed. The couch was still rumpled from being used as a bed. They'd been so close last night. Or had she just been fooling herself?

"Hell, I don't know why I didn't tell you, Charlotte." Mac lifted his arms and clasped his hands behind his head. He wasn't being completely honest, and that knowledge made him more defensive than ever.

"Didn't you think I'd find out?" she implored.

"Sure, I knew you would." Mac's voice sounded more cavalier than he felt. He'd dreaded this moment since he'd opened the door last night and had seen her standing there. Why hadn't he told her earlier?

"I see."

Charlotte looked away, and Mac knew she neither saw . . . nor understood anything. How could she? This must seem like an out-and-out deception to her. But it wasn't. He didn't care if she knew about the money. It was the other things. What woman could love a man who couldn't come to grips with his fears?

"I tried to tell you."

"Really? When?" Charlotte was scared. Something else was wrong. She could sense it. But what could it be?

"Yesterday." Boy, she had those questioning techniques of a mother down pat. Just the right voice inflection, just the right challenging posture. All designed to make you feel as guilty as hell. "I asked you to come out—said I had something to tell you."

"You mean before Elizabeth walked in?" Charlotte asked. Mac nodded.

"So. After knowing me for a over a month and spending the night making love with me, you decided that I should know something about you. How magnanimous of you, Mac." Charlotte tried to keep the hurt from her voice, but she failed miserably. She'd fallen in love with a man she'd thought to be warm and sensitive, but now . . . Had he been playing her for a fool all along?

"What are you doing?" Mac watched as Charlotte bent over collecting her clothes, trying not to notice the captivating curve of bare bottom visible below his sweatshirt. This was no time to let his hormones take over.

"I'm getting dressed." Charlotte smoothed her sweater over her arm. "Would you please direct me to your bathroom?" When he didn't answer, Charlotte headed in the opposite direction from the kitchen.

"There's more."

"What?" Charlotte turned around, staring at him.

"There's more you should know." Mac got up and walked toward the computer in the far corner of the room, trying to ignore the pain in her eyes. "Have you ever heard of Benjamin McQuade?"

"The writer?" Charlotte dropped her clothes across an overstuffed recliner that matched the couch. "The one who wrote *Eden's Surrender*?"

"One in the same."

"I loved that book. After reading it my junior year of high school, I waited for him to write another. The story begged for a sequel."

"But he never wrote another." Mac tossed the copy of *Eden's Surrender* he'd picked out of his bookcase on the desk. His picture—younger, more innocent—stared up at him from the dust jacket.

Suddenly, the fact that she'd never heard Mac's first name registered in her mind. "You're Benjamin McQuade." Even though she knew in her mind that it was true, a part of Charlotte wished he'd tell her he'd been joking. She prayed he'd deny that he'd hidden such an important part of himself from her.

It wasn't a question, but Mac nodded anyway.

Charlotte swallowed and looked from Mac, trying to comprehend all she'd heard this morning. He must have thought her a real country bumpkin. Straight off the turnip truck. Poor, stupid, little Charlotte Handley falling in love with her daughter's English teacher. But who was he really? A world famous author.

Charlotte tried to sound as if her heart wasn't breaking. "Is that how you got all this?" Her hand swept around the room before it dropped to her side. "I seem to recall *Eden's Surrender* was a best seller."

"The royalties certainly didn't hurt my financial situation, but my family had money, old money." Why was he acting so crass? Was he trying to drive her away?

Charlotte blinked back tears till her throat hurt from the effort. "So what are you doing in Williamsburg, Benjamin McQuade? Collecting data for a new book? Are you going to call it, *The Sexy Teacher Meets the Naive Divorcee*?"

"Charlotte." Mac moved around the desk and reached for her hand. Charlotte pulled away.

"I'm sorry. That was a cheap shot. Whatever your reasons for being . . . what do you call this? Incognito? Anyway, they're your own. You don't owe me anything."

"The hell I don't! I thought I made it clear last night how I felt about you." This time when he grabbed for her, he didn't let her jerk away.

"Don't worry, Mr. McQuade. I won't hold you responsible for words spoken in the heat of passion." She was going to cry, Charlotte just knew it. All she wanted to do was get away from him before the waterworks started. She didn't want him to see how hurt she was.

"But I meant it. Damnit, Charlotte, you know I did." Maybe he *should* listen to the old hormones. He'd give her a little taste of what they'd felt last night, what they had every time they got within three feet of each other.

With a hungry need, Mac couldn't deny, he drew Charlotte against him. His lips moved sensuously over hers, his tongue probed the honeyed depths of her mouth, and she—did nothing.

Charlotte fought the urge to wrap her arms around him, to bury her fingers in the silky strands of his hair. His manly scent surrounded her, inundated her senses, weakened her resolve. With the last particle of her strength, she pushed him away. He didn't resist.

"I'm not denying what you do to me. What we do to each other." Charlotte searched his eyes with her own. "And I think you believe what you say about loving me. But love is more than this." She reached up and touched his bottom lip, stifling a gasp when he wet the tip of her finger with his tongue.

"Love is trusting and sharing. I opened up to you, Mac—told you things about myself nobody else knows. But you didn't." Charlotte moved out of his embrace and reached for her clothes. Without a word she took them into the bathroom off the kitchen to put them on.

Taking off his sweatshirt was hard. The soft, worn cotton surrounded her with warmth, and the smell of him. Charlotte almost kept it on. With all his money, Mac could certainly afford another one. He probably wouldn't even miss it, and it would mean so much to her. But she couldn't. Holding her breath to suppress a sob, Charlotte pulled it off, folding it over the side of the bathtub.

After she dressed, Charlotte threw more water on her face and finger combed her wild curls. Brian had never shared his thoughts and feelings with her, but somehow Charlotte had learned to live with that—even accept it. Of course, she hadn't loved Brian, hadn't really cared. With Mac it was different. She couldn't be with him knowing there were parts of himself that he wouldn't share.

Charlotte dried her face and left the bathroom. When she entered the living room again, it appeared as if Mac hadn't moved.

"I want to tell you about myself," Mac said, but he didn't look at her, and he didn't continue.

Charlotte waited, her heart tightening as the seconds passed, and he said nothing. Finally, she could stand it no more. "I know you do, Mac," she whispered as she shrugged into her coat. "Maybe someday you'll be able to."

"At least let me drive you into town." The woman he loved was walking out of his life, and he was letting her.

"That's all right. I can manage." Charlotte reached for the door knob.

"Be reasonable, Charlotte. You got lost last night."

Charlotte turned back and stared, trying to etch a picture of him into her memory. With a sigh she opened the door. "I can see things more clearly this morning."

Mac had no idea how long he remained there, unmoving. He heard her crunch along the walkway, heard her car start and pull away, and still he stood. Yesterday, he'd thought her unreasonable when she'd told him to leave. But today it wasn't she. He was the one that forced them apart with his silence. He might as well have built a brick wall around himself littered with no trespassing signs.

Mac ran his fingers through his hair and headed for the kitchen. He opened the refrigerator door and reached for a beer. Before his hand could touch the bottle, he withdrew it. What in the heck did he think he was doing? He'd tried drowning his sorrows in drink last night, and it hadn't gotten him anywhere.

He poured himself a mug of hot, steaming coffee and walked back into the living room, trying to ignore the magnetic pull of the computer. Picking up the spy novel he'd started last week, Mac cursed the fact that the Redskins game wouldn't start for hours. But then he didn't think even that would take his mind off Charlotte.

She wanted him to share himself wth her. His eyes shot to the computer. *He wasn't certain he could reveal all his fears. Would she even want to know how little control he had over that aspect of his life?* He dropped the book and moved toward the keyboard. *But if he wanted her back, there was no other way. And it was all there—in the computer.* Mac flicked the switch and the monitor came to life.

ELEVEN

"It's snowing!"

Charlotte heard Elizabeth's excited voice as she burst through the front door. Charlotte brushed aside the kitchen curtain and peered outside. Sure enough the pewter grey sky was dotted with lacy white flakes. The fact that they were already sticking to the ground gave testimony to the freezing temperature. Charlotte thought again about calling Sally Reinert and canceling.

"Did you hear me? It's snowing." Elizabeth came into the kitchen shaking sparkling frozen droplets out of her hair.

"The dead could hear you, Elizabeth," Charlotte said but softened her admonishment with a smile. She could hardly fault her daughter's exuberance. Charlotte loved snow, too. Under normal circumstances, she'd be as excited as Elizabeth.

"Looks like the weather men were right this time."

Elizabeth leaned over the sink and looked out the window.

"Looks like." They'd listened to the news Friday night, and heard the forecast of snow for the Virginia Tidewater. Charlotte remembered it distinctly because that was the evening Elizabeth had told her Mac hadn't been to school all week.

"Don't you think you should call him, Mom," Elizabeth had suggested. "He might be sick and have no one to take care of him."

"He's not sick," Charlotte had answered.

"How do you know, Mom?"

"I just do," Charlotte had snapped, but Elizabeth had been undaunted.

"Well, I don't think he'd take off all this time if he weren't sick. He could lose his job, and then what would he do?"

Charlotte had resisted the urge to tell her daughter everything—that she certainly didn't have to waste her time worrying about what Mr. McQuade would do for money. She didn't even have to worry about him being alone. After all, he had Miss Gracie.

"Mom."

Elizabeth's voice brought Charlotte back to the present. She put the glass of milk she'd just poured on the kitchen table. "What?" If Elizabeth had noticed all the times that her mother's mind had wandered since last weekend, she hadn't mentioned it. And for that Charlotte was grateful.

"What time is the Grand Illumination?"

"I'm not sure. We're all supposed to be at Sally's house by five o'clock, then walk down to Duke of Gloucester Street from there."

Charlotte scooped macaroni and cheese onto Elizabeth's plate. "Are you certain you don't want to come along? The invitation clearly stated, 'Charlotte Handley and family.' "

"No. Todd said he'd call tonight. And I really don't feel like going out." Elizabeth put her hamburger in the roll and sat down.

"Okay. Eat your dinner. I better get dressed." The last place Charlotte felt like going was a party, but she'd told Sally weeks ago, when her friend had first planned this Grand Illumination get together, that she'd be there. After all, the world couldn't come to a screeching halt just because Mac didn't love her.

Charlotte examined herself in the mirror. She decided more makeup wouldn't cover the dark circles under her eyes. She simply had to start getting more sleep. *Just realize it's over, and try to forget him.* The problem was, she couldn't. Every day since she'd left his house last Sunday, exactly one week ago, she'd hoped he would call or come by. He hadn't. When she'd found out he'd been absent all week . . . "Admit it, he's kissed this little burg good-bye," she mumbled to herself as she stepped into her winter white corduroy skirt.

Charlotte pulled on her ankle high boots and ran a brush through her hair. "Ready as I'll ever be," she sighed and left the room.

"Elizabeth, I won't be late," Charlotte called from the hallway. "I'm locking the front door."

"Okay, Mom. Have a good time."

"I'm trying," Charlotte told herself as she waited with the hundreds of people who stood on the snow covered grass next to the Powder Magazine for the lighting of the Christmas tree. She shivered, stuffing her glove-clad hands deep into her coat pockets, and wondering where Mac was at this very moment. A cannon blast split the icy night and the giant ever-green blossomed to life, covered with sparkling white lights that seemed to dance in the wind.

The Christmas season had officially arrived in Williamsburg. Someone in the group burst into song, and before long all were serenading the tree with a rousing chorus of "O Tannenbaum." The singing changed to ohs and ahs when the fireworks display began.

"Let's go. On the way back to the party, we can check out the houses that have won blue ribbons," Sally said as she linked her arm through Charlotte's. Every year Colonial Williamsburg awarded prizes to the restored homes that they considered did the best job of decorating for Christmas. Only natural ele-ments could be used, and aside from the single white candle in every window and the porch lights, no gaudy twentieth century features were allowed.

"Are you all right?" Sally asked as they trudged up Duke of Gloucester Street.

"Sure. Maybe a little cold. Oh, look how they used oyster shells to form that wreath," Charlotte answered hoping to change the subject.

Sally stopped and examined the door critically. "I like that. Maybe I'll try it next year on my house. What do you think?"

Charlotte tried to shrug, but she was shivering too much.

"Hey, you are cold." Sally pulled Charlotte along

the sidewalk. "Must be the snow. But it adds a nice touch, don't you think?"

"Great for the Christmas spirit."

It didn't take long for Sally and Doug Reinert's house to fill up with people. Charlotte estimated, conservatively, that Sally had invited half the town to "stop over for eggnog."

Charlotte wandered out of the living room, where a huge Douglas Fir glittered with homemade ornaments, and guests gathered around an upright piano singing carols. The dining room was just as crowded. Charlotte tried to squeeze around an overweight man who wasn't about to give up his spot at the table.

"Great cookies," he said jovially. "Like my mother used to make."

Charlotte smiled and nodded—and left the dining room. "Let's face it," she mumbled to herself as she opened the door to the dark, deserted playroom in the back of the house, "I'm just not ready for this. A week isn't long enough to get over a broken heart." Charlotte picked up a teddy bear that one of Sally's children had left on the floor and wondered if she'd ever get over this heartache.

Charlotte sat down on a toy chest, and gazed out the playroom window. The snow really was lovely— like tiny lace doilies floating to earth. In the background, Charlotte could hear the party noises: the doorbell chimes, someone's forced laughter, the mandatory Christmas carols, but here, in the dark she looked out on the quiet white world and tried not to think.

She felt someone watching her just moments before a weight pressed against her legs.

"This is for you," the lovingly familiar voice said.

Charlotte gaped down at the cardboard box on her lap, then up at Mac. The shoulders of his bomber jacket were covered with snow, and his wind-tossed hair glistened in the dim light from the window. She wanted to grab him, make sure he was real. Instead, she touched the box.

Mac's voice was low, softer than the whispery snow. "You wanted to know me, my secrets, my fears. They're all there, Charlotte, in that box."

Charlotte twined her fingers with Mac's and lead the way up her front walk. He carried the box under his other arm. She still didn't know what it contained, and like Pandora, Charlotte wasn't certain she should find out. Maybe she had been too demanding before. Maybe just having the part of Mac that he wanted to share with her was enough.

"You found her!" Elizabeth opened the front door, beaming her approval before Charlotte even found her key.

"Yeah." Mac stepped inside and tugged on one of Elizabeth's red curls. "She was right where you said she'd be, singing Christmas carols and drinking eggnog."

His blue-green gaze found hers, and Charlotte looked away. He had to know why she'd been sitting all alone in the dark.

"So, you guys didn't stay at the party very long."

"I think it was getting ready to break up," Charlotte lied. "You know how those things are." Actually, she had surprised Sally by announcing she and Mac were leaving.

"Oh, I'd thought you'd be more in the spirit now that *he's* here," her friend had said.

"Did Todd call?" Charlotte asked her daughter while Mac hung up their coats. He'd put the box on the coffee table, and Charlotte tried not to stare at it.

"Yes. We're going to the basketball game Friday night, if it's okay with you."

"Sure, Lizzy."

Mac had come back into the room and the three of them stood, staring at each other. Charlotte was beginning to wonder if they should have gone to Mac's house when Elizabeth cleared her throat.

"Well, I guess I'll go in my room, and . . . study. Yeah, I think I better start studying for finals. They'll be here before I know it, right, Mr. McQuade?"

"You bet, Elizabeth. You can't study too much." His eyes never left Charlotte's face.

"I hate to banish her to her room," Mac said after Elizabeth had disappeared down the hall and the click of her closing door had faded.

"It's all right, she spends a lot of time in there anyway, listening to tapes and . . . I guess she even studies some." Charlotte walked around to the front of the couch. "Would you like to sit down . . . or can I get you something to drink?" It was obvious hospitality wasn't uppermost on her mind. More than a half hour had passed since Mac had walked into the playroom, and with the exception of holding her hand, he had yet to touch her. Charlotte ached for him.

"No. I'm fine." Mac sat down and pulled Charlotte onto the couch beside him. "I missed you this week."

Such simple words, yet they warmed Charlotte's heart as nothing else could. "I missed you, too. About last Sunday, I probably shouldn't have left like—"

"No." Mac's finger brushed against Charlotte's lips, silencing her. "You were right to leave. Everything you said to me was true. And you weren't the first person to say it." His voice gentled. "You were just the first person I cared enough about to listen. I've been afraid, Charlotte." His blue-green gaze searched hers. "Afraid opening up the past would shatter my control."

"Mac, I . . ." Charlotte could tell this was hard for him. She'd been wrong. She didn't need to know everything. All she needed was him.

"Please, Charlotte. I want you to know. I want us to share." He turned to face straight ahead. "Remember when I said that Benjamin McQuade hadn't written anything else?" He seemed to sense her nod. "Well, that wasn't exactly true. He . . . I wrote a book about my experiences in Vietnam."

Mac's laugh was full of self-mockery. "That's not bad, is it? A book every fifteen years?" His expression sobered. "Actually it took less than a year to write, but it took almost thirteen years before I could begin. Then more than a year passed before I had the nerve to let someone else see it."

"Is that what's in the box, your book?" Charlotte's heart beat at jackhammer speed.

Mac looked to the package on the coffee table,

then back to Charlotte. "Yeah. It's a novel, fiction . . . but not really."

"It happened to you," Charlotte whispered.

Mac nodded his head. "Back in 1970, I thought I had the world by the tail. I was young, just out of college, and had a best selling book to my credit. Things had always come easy for me." Mac's gaze met Charlotte's. "You know, the old golden boy syndrome. That was me, the golden boy. I'd even married a golden girl to share the good life with," he added cynically. "My father kept pestering me about my draft status. I'd lost my 2S when I'd graduated, and my lottery number wasn't good. But hey, I was a golden boy. What could happen?

"When Uncle Sam's notice arrived, dad was furious that I hadn't joined the Coast Guard or something, but he still offered to use his influence to keep me stateside." Mac watched for Charlotte's reaction. "Money does have its privileges. But this time I refused to use them.

"The sparkle was wearing off my marriage. Sometimes what appears to be gold, is only a gilt veneer. And besides, Hemingway had been to war, right?"

Mac almost seemed to be talking to himself now. "Charlie, the Viet Cong, didn't seem to realize how important us golden boys were to the free world. I hadn't been in 'Nam more than six months before I was captured." Mac heard Charlotte's sharp intake of breath and stopped.

"You were a P.O.W.?"

"From November sixteenth, 1970, till the C-141 Starlifter with me aboard, taxied into Clark Air Force Base in February of 1973."

"Mac." The word escaped Charlotte on a sob. "How did you stand it?" She'd imagined all sorts of things that could have happened to him, but never this. She remembered seeing pictures of the gaunt, former P.O.W.s disembarking from the plane in the Philippines. A shudder ran through her as she realized she may have even seen Mac on the evening news without realizing who he was.

Mac reached for Charlotte's hand. He hadn't told her about his past to upset her, though he knew it would. But now he wanted more than anything to give her the comfort she'd given him. Slowly, he gathered her close. "Man is able to endure a lot more than he thinks himself capable of." Mac combed his fingers through her curls. "There are techniques you develop . . . strategies that help you get through hard times."

Charlotte tried to brush away the tears that wet his flannel shirt. She raised her head and met his gaze. "Is that what you did, develop strategies?"

"Yeah, I guess I was pretty good at it, too. Because some of them, like not sharing myself, have been almost impossible to shake." He brushed a kiss across her forehead and settled back against the pillows. "I wasn't the same person, when I got back from 'Nam. Carol was the first to notice it."

"Your wife?" Charlotte experienced a slight pang of jealousy.

"Yeah, she'd moved out of our house when word hit the states that I was missing in action. When I got back, she surfaced long enough to tell me I'd changed, and hand me the divorce papers."

Charlotte's fist knotted in his shirt. "What kind of woman was she to do such a thing?"

"Hey, take it easy." Mac straightened out the flannel. "I told you before that it was for the best. Besides, Carol was a realist, the reality being, I was a mess."

"Well, she should have tried to help you," Charlotte said with fire in her sky-blue eyes.

"It wasn't in her to do that. Hell, if she had, I'd have probably ended up in worse shape than I was," Mac laughed. "Suffice it to say that we should never have gotten married in the first place, and Carol did the smart, if not exactly the most humanitarian thing, by leaving when she did."

"If you say so." Charlotte leaned back against his chest and heard his rumbling laughter.

"I love it when you act like a protective shewolf."

Charlotte slapped at the soggy shirt. "Oh, I was doing no such thing."

"Besides, I had plenty of people trying to help. Both of my parents had passed away while I was in 'Nam." Charlotte felt his arm tighten around her, and knew that bothered him. "But the V.A. was great, and my uncle—"

"The one who's a Mafia kingpin?"

Mac laughed again. "The same. Though I think you should know that in his spare time he's a U.S. senator."

"You're kidding?" Now Charlotte was laughing.

"No, ma'am. I wouldn't joke about something that serious." Mac rested his chin on the top of Charlotte's head. "Well, anyway, they all did their level best to make me start feeling something again, but I couldn't. In the camps I'd worked so hard not to feel or think . . ." He shook his head. "Anyway it was hard to break that habit."

"Is that when you moved to Williamsburg?"

"Hmmm. I'd gone to school here and enjoyed the town. The teaching job . . . well, I just kind of fell into that, and discovered I liked it.

"Yeah, I was living a pretty satisfactory life, in a superficial kind of way, till this redhead walked into my classroom and started stirring everything up."

Charlotte sat up, her spine straight. "If you're referring to me, I never did one thing to get you stirred up, as you so eloquently put it."

"Maybe not on purpose you didn't, but I've got to tell you, lady, you've had me agitated since the first moment I saw you."

Mac leaned forward and kissed the lips he'd been longing to caress all evening. A low, satisfied groan rumbled through his chest when Charlotte opened for him. His tongue whisked inside her mouth, tasting the warm honey he'd come to know as Charlotte.

"Mac." Charlotte tried to catch her breath.

"Mmmm." Her neck tasted as good as her mouth.

"May I read your book?"

Mac sat up. "That's what I brought it for, but you want to read it *now?*"

Charlotte smiled at his expression. "With Elizabeth in the next room, I think it might be the best course of action."

"Oh, yeah, I forgot." Mac removed his hands from beneath Charlotte's wool sweater. "It's a long manuscript."

He wasn't having second thoughts, was he? "I'm

a fast reader." Charlotte wriggled off the couch before he could stop her. "Just let me get my glasses."

Charlotte found them in her pocketbook and lifted the manuscript box onto her lap. Almost reverently she opened the lid and read the title page.

A Vietnam Experience by Benjamin McQuade.

Her heart swelled with pride. "I like the title." Charlotte glanced over toward him. Mac had moved against the far end of the couch, and watched her intently.

"There are probably a lot of typos and things, maybe I should polish it up first before you read it."

He *was* having second thoughts. Well, Charlotte wasn't going to let him do any backsliding. "Don't worry, I'll take that into consideration while I'm reading. Why don't you just rest?"

"Yeah, maybe I'll take a nap or something." Mac scrunched down on the couch and shut his eyes.

Charlotte turned the page.

This book is dedicated to the brave men and women who lived the Vietnam experience. She liked that, too. Charlotte's eyes skimmed lower.

"Mac!"

"What?" He feigned waking up, but Charlotte knew he hadn't been asleep. Her vision of him was blurred by tears.

"You mentioned me in the dedication."

"Well, I'd hoped you'd like it." He sounded embarrassed.

"I did. Thank you."

"Anytime." He closed his eyes again, and Charlotte began reading the manuscript in earnest.

When the mantel clock struck ten, Charlotte's eyes

felt heavy. She glanced over at Mac. He really was asleep this time. He breathed through his mouth and every once in a while he made a noise very closely resembling a snore. She longed to lie down beside him. And she would . . . as soon as she finished this chapter.

At two o'clock, Charlotte's head fell forward, waking her up. She rubbed her eyes and looked down at the page. How could she have fallen asleep when the main character was in such a tight fix?

By four o'clock M-16s were shooting off in her head, but she was almost finished and couldn't possibly stop reading.

"Charlotte? Charlotte, sweetheart?"

Slowly, painfully, Charlotte tried opening her eyes. Glaring bright sunlight reflected off the snow, streamed through the window and exploded inside her head. She had to get to Mac, had to save Mac.

A gentle hand soothed her brow, brushed away a tangle of hair. Mac. He was there, blocking the torturing light. And he was safe.

Frantically, Charlotte wrapped her arms around his neck, burying her face in his warm chest. "Oh, Mac, I had the most awful dream. You were trapped, so alone, and I tried to get to you . . . I did."

Her body shifted. Instinctively, Charlotte grabbed for the box that started to fall off her lap. Reality invaded her sleep-deprived brain. "It wasn't a dream. Mac, it happened . . . to you."

Mac set the empty box on the floor and gathered Charlotte onto his lap. He'd awakened just moments ago to find her sitting on the couch, asleep, her head bent at an awkward angle. "It's all over now, Charlotte. All over." He felt her body relax against him and smiled. "For goodness sakes, Charlotte, I didn't expect you to stay up all night reading."

"I couldn't put it down." Charlotte sat up. "Your book, it's wonderful." She nestled back against his chest. "What are you going to do with it now?"

Mac leaned back against the pillows. His back was stiff. The couch wasn't nearly long enough for him. But as bad as he felt, Mac knew Charlotte felt worse. He massaged her neck. "I called Sid Green the beginning of the week. He's my agent," Mac explained. "He wanted me to send the manuscript right away. As a matter of fact he offered to fly down and pick it up." Laughter rumbled in his chest. "But I told him my most important critic had to read it first."

"Well, you can tell him she loved it." Charlotte's voice sounded drowsy. Resting against Mac's solid warmth, hearing the strong, steady beat of his heart, feeling his gentle hands was so relaxing.

"Charlotte?"

"Mmmm?"

"Are you falling asleep?"

"Mmmm."

Mac kissed the top of her head. "Do you think you can stay awake long enough to answer a question for me?"

"Sure." Didn't he know she'd do anything for him? Charlotte slowly tilted her head and pressed her lips to the underside of Mac's jaw. His skin bristled with unshaven whiskers and tasted slightly salty.

"Would you marry me?"

"What?" All thoughts of Mr. Sandman fled her

mind. Charlotte jerked away from her comfortable nest and stared Mac in the eye. Had she heard him correctly?

Mac stared back. He'd been hoping for a mellow sleep-induced yes. Apparently she hadn't been that sleepy. "I know you don't think you want to marry again, but this is different. You can still be independent if you want. Finish school, be a librarian. I'm not like . . . well, I won't make you change."

Did he think she didn't know that? Charlotte touched Mac's cheek. "What about Elizabeth? It's not easy being the parent of a teenager."

Mac grinned. Now that the shock of his question was wearing off, Charlotte looked a whole lot more accessible. "I think I can manage it. Of course, I had thought it might be nice if we gave her a little brother or sister, just so I could learn all the aspects of the job. But after all, I'm used to handling thirty adolescents at a time. And since I won't be doing that anymore . . ."

"You've quit teaching?"

"I prefer to call it an extended leave of absence. There have been ideas for books running around in my head for a long time. I just couldn't seem to get started, at least not until I'd finished with that." Mac pointed toward the neat stack of papers on the floor. "Now I want to give myself the chance."

After reading his book last night, Charlotte knew he deserved that chance. He'd been born to write. She leaned forward, tracing the outline of his firm lips with her finger. His arms tightened around her and Charlotte could feel the strength of his leashed passion.

"So?" Mac croaked, pulling away while he still

could. She was doing strange and wonderful things to his equilibrium. "Are you going to marry me? You know I love you with all my heart." A new thought entered his mind. "If it's the money, I can give it away."

"Let's don't be ridiculous."

"Yeah, well, I was kind of hoping you wouldn't insist on that," Mac laughed.

"Are you two still out here?" Elizabeth scuffed into the room, scratching her head, her untied bathrobe dragging behind her like a train.

Charlotte smiled at the sight her daughter made but didn't move from her spot on Mac's lap.

Mac didn't feel the slightest bit embarrassed either. His arms remained around Charlotte, and he turned to see Elizabeth better. "I'm trying to convince your mother to marry me, and she's a stubborn woman."

"M-o-m!" Elizabeth scurried around to the front of the couch.

"Bringing in the heavy artillery, are you?" Charlotte teased Mac.

"You bet." The sparkle in his blue-green eyes told her he was confident of her response.

"Well, I suppose a wedding would be nice. Around Christmas time?" Charlotte cocked her head.

"Anytime you say, as long as it's soon."

Charlotte shifted slightly and realized that there was more than one reason that Mac had kept her on his lap. She gazed into his eyes. "I love you, Mac, and I want more than anything to marry you. I just have one small condition."

* * *

"How do I look?"

Charlotte examined her daughter thoughtfully. From the toes of her black, patent leather pumps to the simple lines of her emerald green dress, to her curly red hair, her daughter was lovely. Charlotte reached over and straightened the small wreath of holly leaves nestled in Elizabeth's curls. "Beautiful," Charlotte announced. "You look beautiful."

"Hey, Mom. You're the one who's looking beautiful. If you want to know."

"Thank you, Lizzy. I feel beautiful." Charlotte straightened the skirt of her cream-colored silk dress and picked up the nosegay of white roses intertwined with glossy green holly berries that matched Elizabeth's crown. "I guess it's about time to get started."

"Do you think he did it?" Elizabeth asked with barely repressed curiosity.

"I don't know. He never mentioned it again after that day . . . and neither did I." Charlotte thought again of the morning almost three weeks ago when Mac had asked her to marry him, and of the silly request she'd made. When Mac had stopped laughing, he'd kissed her soundly, right in front of her daughter.

"Run off and get dressed, Elizabeth," he'd said. "We'll go have breakfast at Christianna Campbell's to celebrate."

"I have to go to school," Elizabeth had complained.

"That's right. I forgot what day it was. How about tonight?" He'd looked at Charlotte. "Do you have to work?" When she shook her head, he'd asked. "Want to let me escort the two prettiest ladies in town to dinner?"

After Elizabeth had run off to her room, laughing, Mac had kissed Charlotte's forehead. "I'll bet I know what you'd like."

Charlotte had wiggled closer. "Mmmm, you do?" She smiled at his quick intake of breath.

"I was referring to a good ten hours in bed."

Charlotte traced his bottom lip with her tongue. "So was I."

In all the ensuing activity of preparing for the wedding and Christmas, Charlotte had all but forgotten her request.

"Well, I think he wore it," Elizabeth insisted as the music began echoing through Wren Chapel.

Charlotte's hands grasped the plastic handle of her bouquet. "I guess we'll find out in a minute." She leaned over and planted a fleeting kiss on her daughter's cheek. "I love you, Lizzy."

Charlotte and Mac had chosen the Wren Chapel on the William and Mary campus because it was small and intimate. As Charlotte followed her daughter up the aisle she was glad they had. The old, mellow, wood was trimmed with pine and holly, and giant poinsettias decorated the front altar.

Smiling faces caught her eye, as her gaze swept over the wedding guests. Some were dear and familiar, her mother, her sister, Mary Ellen. Others she'd just met, Mac's uncle, Senator Dodson, Sid Green and his wife, friends of Mac's from the V.A hospital.

Charlotte focused on the man waiting for her at the alter. She didn't think she'd ever tire of just looking at him, being with him. He grinned, dimples flashing, and Charlotte floated the last few steps to his side. *He remembered.*

Holding hands, Charlotte and Mac solemnly exchanged their wedding vows, promising to love, honor, and cherish each other. When the minister announced that Mac could kiss the bride, Charlotte's gaze drifted down from her new husband's face.

What she saw made her eyes sparkle. He had worn it. Handing Elizabeth her bouquet, Charlotte reached out and grabbed Mac's tie. "I love you, Benjamin McQuade," she murmured just before she pulled on the cloth fish, bringing Mac's lips down to meet hers.

SHARE THE FUN . . .
SHARE YOUR NEW-FOUND TREASURE!!

You don't want to let your new book out of your sight? That's okay. Your friends can get their own. Order below.

No. 5 A LITTLE INCONVENIENCE by Judy Christenberry
Never one to give up easily, Liz overcomes every obstacle Jason throws in her path and loses her heart in the process.

No. 6 CHANGE OF PACE by Sharon Brondos
Police Chief Sam Cassidy was everyone's protector but could he protect himself from the green-eyed temptress?

No. 7 SILENT ENCHANTMENT by Lacey Dancer
She was elusive and she was beautiful. Was she real? She was Alex's true-to-life fairy-tale princess.

No. 8 STORM WARNING by Kathryn Brocato
The tempest on the outside was mild compared to the raging passion of Valerie and Devon—and there was no warning!

No. 9 PRODIGAL LOVER by Margo Gregg
Bryan is a mystery. Could he be Keely's presumed dead husband?

No. 10 FULL STEAM by Cassie Miles
Jonathan's a dreamer—Darcy is practical. An unlikely combo!

No. 11 BY THE BOOK by Christine Dorsey
Charlotte and Mac give parent-teacher conference a new meaning.

No. 12 BORN TO BE WILD by Kris Cassidy
Jenny shouldn't get close to Garrett. He'll leave too, won't he?